Murder in the Middle

(A Susan Wiles Schoolhouse Mystery)

by

Diane Weiner

For information, e-mail **Cozy Cat Press**, cozycatpress@aol.com or visit our website at: www.cozycatpress.com

COZY CAT
P R E S S

ISBN: 978-1-939816-58-0

Printed in the United States of America

Cover design by Katherine Janda
http://tnjb-art.tumblr.com/

1 2 3 4 5 6 7 8 9 10

This book is dedicated to my husband Robert for listening to endless drafts of my work, sitting through critique groups, proofreading, and being my biggest fan. He truly is the wind beneath my wings.

Chapter 1

Susan Wiles poured herself a second cup of coffee and went back to work on the crossword puzzle. That was one of the perks of being retired. She didn't have to rush in the mornings. The days stretched out like endless ribbons of taffy. Knitting, scrapbooking, and vegan cooking hadn't captured her interest like she'd imagined back when she was still teaching. She opened the blinds to let in the light, but in the midst of a Hudson Valley winter, the sun came out late and lazily, if at all.

The sound of her cellphone startled her. *Who would be calling this early?* It was Principal Antonio Petrocelli, her friend and former colleague, begging her to come down to his school—immediately. It was urgent.

"Antonio, what's wrong? Are you hurt? Did something happen at school?"

"I need your help but I can't talk about it over the phone. Just hurry."

What could be wrong? The last help she gave Antonio was when she'd cleared him as a murder suspect. That was before he became a principal. Is that the kind of help he needed?

Susan rushed through the doors of Westbrook Middle School. When she got inside, her heart beating like a metronome set to presto, she heard the sound of muffled voices in the bookkeeper's office. She entered and let out a gasp, announcing her arrival to Antonio and his secretary.

"Antonio, what happened here?" asked Susan. Papers and file folders littered the floor of the tiny office. The phone receiver hung over the desk, attached to its base like a bungee cord. A framed photo with an ominous looking crack across the glass had been knocked off the shelf of the credenza.

"I... I don't know. I came in this morning and found this." Antonio personified the cliché—he was tall, dark, and extremely handsome. He opened his arms to point out the mess like a hawk flaunting its wing span. "The door was unlocked and the light was on. I'm hoping there's some explanation—that maybe Sophie just had some sort of emergency."

The secretary's caffeinated words tumbled out of her mouth. "But her purse. It's sitting there on the desk. She wouldn't have left without her purse, and her car. Her car's parked outside in the faculty lot. I already called the police. Oh my God! I hope she's okay. We have to find her."

"Try not to panic yet. Like I said, maybe she just left in a hurry and forgot her purse. We checked the campus but I'm sure there are places we've missed," said Antonio.

Susan knew that Antonio didn't believe that. Otherwise he wouldn't have called her. Within moments, two detectives entered the room. Detective Jackson Simpson was paunchy, with a receding hairline. His breath smelled like Doritos.

His partner was country girl pretty and sported a blond ponytail. She turned to Susan.

"Mom, what are you doing here?" she asked. Susan saw disapproval in her daughter's chestnut eyes.

"I was invited. Antonio called me and asked for my help."

"As soon as I saw this mess, I immediately thought of your Mom," said Antonio. "Remember how she solved Vicky's murder back when I was at the elementary school? Right after she retired from teaching music?"

Am I imagining it, or did Lynette just roll her eyes at me? thought Susan. Lynette didn't seem to mind her mother's help when she was pregnant and on bed rest last year, no, siree. She'd been nothing but supportive as Susan investigated and eventually cracked that murder case wide open. Now she was back to being annoyed whenever Susan offered her help. With a baby at home, she should appreciate her mother lending a hand.

Detective Jackson Simpson, Lynette's longtime partner, bent down with his camera and photographed a fast food cup lying under the desk chair. Ice and soda had spilled out onto the floor.

"Hey, Lynette. Maybe we can get some DNA off of that straw," said Jackson.

Susan thought he was an idiot for not recognizing the unlikelihood of Sophie having shared her drink with her abductor, but she held her tongue. Abductor? *This certainly has the hallmark of an abduction,* she thought. *Wasn't there an unsolved abduction in Westbrook less than a year ago?*

Jackson continued to photograph the scene, while Lynette questioned Antonio.

"Her full name is Sophie Bartolo. She was still here when I left last night around five. From the parking lot, I could tell she was the only one there. All the other offices were dark."

"Yes. Lots of times she stayed late on Thursdays to finish payroll," added the secretary.

"How long has she worked here at Westbrook Middle?" asked Lynette.

"Ten years. She started here the same year I did. She should have listened to me. I always told her, 'Finish before dark so you won't have to navigate the winding mountain roads,' offered the secretary. "Something's wrong—I can feel it."

"It looks like there was a struggle, based on the condition of this office," declared Lynette. "I'll get the CSI team over here to give it the once over. Jackson and I'll go back to the station and call her family. Maybe they know where she is. This can't be considered a missing person case yet. It's too soon."

Too soon? What if Sophie was kidnapped? Susan knew that the first twenty four hours were crucial in a kidnapping. By waiting they might miss something important. She followed Lynette out of the office.

"You know, I forgot to ask Antonio what time he needed me to help with the book fair tomorrow. Go on. Kiss Annalise for me. I'll call you later," said Susan. Annalise was Susan's precious gem of a granddaughter.

As a precaution, Jackson sealed the room with yellow crime scene tape. Susan wanted to steal another look at the office after the police were gone. She chastised herself for quitting her yoga classes. Bending underneath that tape wouldn't be an easy task.

Lynette called to her from down the hall. "And Mom, don't even think about going back and contaminating the crime scene."

Susan followed Antonio into his office. When they were alone, she asked him if he had any gut reactions as to who the perpetrator might be.

"I have no idea," said Antonio. "She mostly keeps to herself. She lost her husband in a freaky hiking accident last year. I haven't heard her talk about any other family members. She's been spending time with one of our math teachers—Mitch Coniglio."

"Did she hang out with anyone else here at work?"

"She eats with our guidance counselor most days. You could talk to her." Antonio clasped Susan's hands in his. It was like a scene in a movie. "Please help me, Susan. We don't want parents and staff questioning our safety protocols. You know how schools work. Maybe you could quietly solve this before it blows up into a big police matter."

Susan liked Antonio and respected his leadership, however, he had an ego the size of Jupiter. She knew he was worried about this reflecting badly on him and couldn't wait 24-48 hours for the police to determine this was a crime. After all, he was the principal—and a new one at that. He'd recently been transferred here from Westbrook Elementary.

"I'll do my best," said Susan. She felt that familiar tingle in her stomach that she got whenever she started working on a case. Sleuthing was the one hobby that greatly enhanced her enjoyment of retirement. She was good at it, and it gave her a purpose.

On the way to her Prius, Susan noticed something shiny in the dirty snow that flanked the parking lot. She carefully picked it up and examined it. It was a silver ID bracelet with the name Caleb engraved into it. A link looked as though it had been forcefully broken. She wrapped it in a tissue and put it in her purse. It was a longshot, but maybe the owner of this bracelet had something to do with this case.

Chapter 2

Mike, Susan's husband of nearly forty years, was still at work. It was just her and her two cats, Ludwig and Johann, in the house today. The smell of burnt coffee greeted her as soon as she opened the front door and she realized that she'd left the coffee maker on in her haste to get to the school this morning. She grabbed a muffin—a low-fat bran muffin—and sat down at the dining room table to plan her investigation.

Susan carefully took the bracelet out of her purse. How did it wind up in the faculty parking lot? It could be nothing. But what if it was an important clue? She could start by figuring out who Caleb was. She knew she should turn the bracelet in to the police soon just in case it turned out to be evidence, but first she wanted to have a closer look at it. Maybe she should be wearing gloves, just in case there were prints. Too late now.

It was solid silver. The links were sturdy and thick, except for the one that had been broken. It would have taken some force to break that link. Did it happen during a struggle? Susan went to the computer and found the faculty page on the Westbrook Middle School website. There wasn't anyone named Caleb on the list. She copied down the name of the guidance counselor. Didn't Antonio's secretary say that Sophie often ate lunch with her? That might be a place to start. Surely the police would interview her, but Susan had a way of drawing information out of people.

Susan began searching for Sophie Bartolo on the internet, but was interrupted by a knock at the door. She had forgotten that the repair man was scheduled to come by today and take a look at her anemic clothes dryer.

"Good afternoon, ma'am. Woulda been here earlier, but there was a traffic jam down the road. A couple of police cars blocked off the road by the school over there on Vineyard Avenue."

"I wonder what's going on there," said Susan. "Was there an accident?"

"Don't think so. It looks like maybe something happened around the school. Odd though. We sure don't have much crime in Westbrook."

"No," said Susan. "Just a couple of murder cases that made the headlines last year." Susan was surprised that the three separate murder cases hadn't registered as crime in the repair man's world. She hoped her sarcasm hadn't registered either.

"Yeah. And that kidnapping case. It still hasn't been solved I don't think. That poor girl's still missing and it's been—what? Six months or so?"

"You mean the bank teller? She went missing after work, right?"

"That's the one. They never talked about a ransom note or nothing. I'm sure she's long gone, the poor girl." The repair man checked the lint filter, then pulled the dryer out from the wall. "Looks like you need to replace the heating element. I'll order the part and we'll give you a call when it comes in. It'll work good as new."

"Thank you. At least we don't have to buy a new dryer." She showed him out and sat back down at the computer. Just as she was about to get to work again, her phone rang.

"Hi, Mike. The repair man just left." She filled him in on the dryer repair, but not the events of the morning. She knew he'd start admonishing her to leave the bookkeeper's disappearance to the police. He was as bad as Lynette. They were always worried that she'd get herself into danger. She'd tell him tonight over dinner. *It's almost 3:00. Maybe I'll drop by the school and see if I can have a chat with the guidance counselor. Oh, and I can drop off the bracelet at the police station.*

Chapter 3

At the police station, Lynette and Jackson assembled the information they had on Sophie Bartolo and decided to enlist the media's help by putting out a description and picture. Sophie's parents hadn't heard from her and were convinced she'd been taken against her will. Jackson typed: "Sophie Bartolo is forty years old, five foot four, approximately 150 pounds. She has brown eyes and curly black hair."

"How's that sound?" asked Jackson.

"Wouldn't get many hits on Match.com, but sounds accurate. Hopefully someone saw her and can tell us something. Let's open an anonymous tip line too."

"Lynette, do you think this is related to that bank teller who went missing last summer? That woman was about the same age as Sophie Bartolo. As a matter of fact, they even look alike—dark hair, slightly plump."

"We can't rule it out. That crossed my mind too. We haven't gotten a ransom note yet. Sophie's parents are heartbroken. They're driving in from Rhode Island and will be here tonight. She's their only child."

"I can't imagine what they must be going through. Lynette, remember that other case in Marlboro a few months ago? As far as we know, their police department is still investigating, but the trail must be cold by now. They had a witness who saw someone grab that dental hygienist and drive away with her in a white van."

"Yes, I remember. Marlboro is only a few towns away from us. Could be the same perp. Let's pull up the report."

Jackson quickly found the information and skimmed through it. The dental hygienist was slightly younger than Sophie, but also a brunette, and with a similar build. She'd been abducted as she was leaving work. One of the patients in the office had walked across the street to Rite Aid to fill a prescription the dentist had given him. When he came out of the drugstore, he'd seen the girl being shoved into the back of the van.

Lynette read over his shoulder for several minutes. "But look, it says the witness may not have been very reliable. He'd just had some major dental work, and they'd given him some pain meds before he left the office. In any case, they never found the van or the victim."

"Yeah, but we don't have much else to go on at this point. I've been on pain medication before. You still know what's going on. That's two unsolved missing person's cases in a short time. Sophie Bartolo makes three. More than a coincidence, don't you think? Let's get over to Sophie's house and see if we can find anything there." Jackson grabbed their jackets from the coat rack. A bag of barbecue potato chips stuck halfway out of his pocket. "I'll drive."

When Lynette and Jackson arrived, they canvassed Sophie's house and yard before going inside. Nothing looked unusual. The front door was locked and the lights were off. They started in the kitchen. An empty coffee mug and yesterday's newspaper were on the kitchen table. The refrigerator sported a photo of Sophie with a smiling blond man wearing a Santa hat.

"This may be a boyfriend," said Lynette. She removed the photo from the fridge. Lynette followed Jackson into the bedroom where they found a framed picture of the couple on the nightstand next to Sophie's bed. "Yep, I'd say boyfriend."

Jackson checked the bathroom. "Here's a man's electric shaver and a second toothbrush," said Jackson. "Boyfriend for sure."

Lynette went into the living room and turned on the computer, which opened to Sophie's e-mail. The messages were mostly store advertisements, but one caught her eye.

"Look, Jackson. This seems to be a threat of some sort. It says, *don't think you'll get away with it. I'll never let you rest.*"

"Now that does sound like a threat," said Jackson. It was sent by *revenger1@gmail.com.*" Jackson scrolled back through the e-mails. "Look. There are two similar messages." Lynette looked over his shoulder.

"We can trace them, but I'll bet whoever sent it wasn't dumb enough to send it from his own computer."

"So, we're most likely looking at either a stalker, or a serial kidnapper with a preference for brunettes," said Jackson.

"Until we find something else, we'll go with that. Let's go to the school and talk to the guidance counselor."

"Sounds like a plan," said Lynette.

Chapter 4

Susan crouched behind the bushes and watched Lynette and Jackson leave, before entering the school. She scratched her hand on a dry branch. Lynette would lecture her about sticking her nose into police business if she saw her and she wasn't in the mood to hear it. She wished Lynette could understand that solving crimes kept her mind active and made her feel useful. She wasn't trying to do Lynette's job; she just wanted to help, especially now that Lynette had a baby to take care of.

"Your daughter and her partner just left," said Antonio. "They interviewed my secretary and the guidance counselor, Elaine Cummings. I'm so glad you're willing to help me. It's not that I don't have faith in the police department, it's just that they have a full plate and can't devote one hundred percent of their time to this like I know you will."

"Always the charmer, Antonio." Susan gave him a squeeze around the shoulders. "Antonio, do you have anyone on staff named Caleb? Maybe even a delivery man or maintenance worker?"

"No, I can't think of anyone named Caleb. Why?"

"Never mind. Can I speak with Miss Cummings?"

"Sure. Her office is right around the corner."

Susan knocked on Elaine Cummings' door and was invited to have a seat. The office was slightly larger than Sophie's. A black, microfiber sofa faced the oak desk. Susan detected the faint aroma of lavender.

"Miss Cummings, I'm trying to help find Sophie. My name is Susan Wiles. I understand you were friends."

"Please call me Elaine. Yes, we're friends. I'm worried sick about her."

"I know you've already spoken to the police, but Antonio asked if I'd lend my assistance as well. As far as you know, did anyone want to harm Sophie? Did she have any co-workers with whom she didn't get along?"

"She was—I mean is—quiet. She mostly stays to herself; she's not overly friendly, but I don't know of anyone who…" Elaine paused. "Wait a minute. There was something. One day last week, I walked into her office and I heard her talking on the phone. She sounded upset—told whoever it was never to bother her again. I don't think it was just a telemarketer. I asked her about it, but she said she didn't want to talk about it."

"Maybe it was an old boyfriend or something. Was she seeing anyone?"

"Like I told the police, she'd been seeing one of the math teachers here for the past few months. They seemed happy. His name's Mitch Coniglio."

Susan made a mental note of the name and leaned forward in her seat. "What can you tell me about her family? Were they close?"

"Her parents live in Rhode Island. Sophie's an only child. She was married, you know. Poor thing. Her husband, Adam, had a terrible accident. Sophie was with him when he died. They were on a picnic up at Lake Minnewaska. They went on a hike and he fell over the edge of a waterfall. He died immediately."

"How awful. Poor Sophie. How do you recover from something like that?"

"To make things worse, there were rumblings that she deliberately pushed him. Something about him being afraid of heights and how he never would have gotten that close to the edge. Sophie would never have done something like that. Ridiculous. It's been over two years now. Mitch is the first man she's been out with since Adam's death. I took that as a sign she was progressing in the healing process."

Spoken like a true guidance counselor, thought Susan. "Is there any chance Sophie would have just felt the need to get away for a while? That she went voluntarily?"

"Without her purse or for that matter, her car? No way."

"Thanks, Elaine. I'll see if I can find anything. You know, that blond police detective you spoke to earlier is my daughter, Lynette." Saying that still made Susan beam with pride, the same way she beamed when she told people her son Evan was a medical student.

"I know. I remember seeing you both together on the news last year after the murder case at the high school was solved. Looked like you were quite the team. She was pregnant then."

"Yes, she was." Susan whipped out her phone. "Here's a picture of my beautiful granddaughter, Annalise. She's walking now." Susan was always ready to show off her grandbaby. She'd even learned how to take videos on her phone and how to post pictures on Facebook.

"My Lord, how beautiful," said Elaine. "Look at those blond waves, just like grandma."

Susan wondered where her own blond waves came from. She had no idea what her birth mother looked like. The parents she grew up with both had dark hair.

"She got the blond hair from Lynette, and the waves from Jason, her Daddy. Jason is already showing her addition facts on flashcards and speaking to her in

French. He's really into education, being a college professor and all."

"Enjoy her. You know how fast they grow. And thanks for trying to help. The quicker Sophie is found, the better. I'm trying not to think about what situation she may be in right now. This used to be a safe little town. We moved up here when the kids were about to start school because New York City had too much crime. Here, we could raise our kids in a safe environment and Bob could hop on the train and commute to his job. Nice being a stone's throw away from the big city."

"Westbrook is still a great little town. We'll find Sophie." Susan hoped she was right. On her way home, she pulled into the parking lot of the two-story, brick police station to drop off the bracelet. *Maybe,* she thought, *if she talked fast, Lynette wouldn't be able to butt in with questions about the delay in reporting it.*

"Lynette, I found something in the parking lot this morning. It probably has nothing to do with Sophie's disappearance, but I thought you'd want to see it just in case." Susan took the bracelet out of her purse and spilled it onto Lynette's desk. "One of the links is broken. I found it in the parking lot."

"Looks like a bracelet."

"I already checked the faculty roster, and I asked Antonio if he knew anyone named Caleb associated with the school. No luck."

"Mom, did you wear gloves when you picked it up? I'll bet you ruined any possibility of getting fingerprints off of it. And what took you so long to bring it over here?"

"Well, Kinsey Malone has been hard at work I see," said Jackson. He strolled into Lynette's office, a bag of Fritos in hand.

"Maybe you should have been doing the footwork yourself, Gomer Pyle." Jackson always sided with Lynette and made it clear that Susan's help wasn't needed or appreciated.

"The guy Sophie was dating is named Mitch, so it doesn't belong to him," said Lynette. "It had to have been dropped recently, since the snowplows cleaned up after the storm the other day. It would have gotten swept away."

"Wasn't there a kidnapping case just a few months ago? The media was all over it for a while, but I haven't heard anything about it in weeks."

"We're looking into it," said Jackson. "There was also an unsolved case in Marlboro last year. Could be the same guy."

Susan glanced at her watch. "I'd better get going. Mike'll be home soon and I should do something about starting dinner."

"I'll be wrapping up here soon too. The daycare closes at six," said Lynette.

"Hey, Gomer. Tell your beautiful fiancé I said hello."

"I'll be sure to tell Theresa," said Jackson.

Chapter 5

Susan heard the sound of the key opening the front door. Even after spending decades together, her heart still gave a little flutter in anticipation of seeing Mike.

"Hi, Hon. How was your day?" asked Mike. He sat his lunchbox on the kitchen counter and gave Susan a kiss. She ruffled his wavy brown hair. Mike had the same chestnut eyes as Lynette and was handsome in a rugged, trustworthy sort of way. He worked in the building permits office down at City Hall.

"What's for dinner?" he asked. He took the lid off the saucepan that was beginning to boil over on the front burner of the stove.

"That's couscous," said Susan. "I have tofu baking in the oven." Susan knew he'd rather be eating lasagna and French fries—so would she—but they'd been sticking to their healthy eating plan for quite a while already and she'd tried her best to keep the momentum going. Mike had lost twenty pounds since they started. Susan had gained five. She chose to blame it on aging rather than her affinity for Mint Milanos and cookie dough ice cream.

"Antonio Petrocelli called me this morning." She proceeded to fill him in on the events of the day. "We're thinking the owner of the bracelet, Caleb, or else the same person responsible for two other abductions may be responsible."

"Is that *we* as in *you and the police department?*"

"Well, of course. I'm the one who found the bracelet, you know." Susan recognized a defensiveness in the tone of her own voice.

"Just be careful. I don't want to be putting out an Amber Alert for my wife."

After dinner, Susan looked on the internet for information about Sophie Bartolo and Mitch Coniglio. She found Sophie's marriage license, and an obituary for her late husband, Adam Bartolo. *Poor man was only 38 years old,* thought Susan. According to the obituary, Adam was survived by his wife, his parents, and a brother. Then, she searched for silver identification bracelets. They were available on many different websites, and, of course, in jewelry stores. Trying to find the source of this particular bracelet was next to impossible.

Mike sat down next to her on the sofa. "You might try the local jewelry stores," said Mike. "Caleb isn't a very common name. It's possible someone might remember engraving it."

"That's a good idea. There are only two jewelry stores in town. It's a longshot, but worth pursuing."

Having finished with the case for the evening, she went on her adoption website. Over a year ago, she'd been blindsided with the news that she'd been adopted. After the death of the woman who Susan thought was her mother, she'd found adoption papers—her own adoption papers—in a safety deposit box at the bank. Having support from others in the same boat had proven to be invaluable. Thank goodness for the internet. She'd been searching on and off for her birth parents this past year, but every avenue she'd explored had led to a dead end. In a way, that had been a relief. She had reservations about opening this can of worms at her age. On the other hand, her curiosity wouldn't allow her to let it rest. She wondered if she'd gotten that nosy streak from her birth mother. The mom who'd raised her would have let sleeping dogs lie.

Chapter 6

The next morning, Susan headed for the jewelry stores. The first stop was a quaint Mom and Pop shop in downtown Westbrook. The area was kept in pristine condition. Renovations were made when needed and the buildings were scrupulously clean. Susan loved Westbrook because it reminded her of a New England resort town. Her boots tap-danced across the cobblestones and into the store.

"If it isn't Susan Wiles. Haven't seen you in a while. Is that wristwatch acting up again?" The owner was an elderly gentleman with a thick head of gray hair and a soft, weathered face.

"No, T.J. My watch has kept ticking along ever since you changed the battery for me."

"Then how can I help you?" He looked down at her wedding ring. "Let me shine that up for you while you're here." He placed the ring in a steam cleaner.

"Thanks. Got to bring Mike around so you can shine his up too. Do you happen to sell silver identity bracelets? You know, the kind that you engrave?"

"Sure do. Are you in the market?"

"Not at the moment. I found one in the parking lot of the middle school. It's engraved with the name Caleb. I'd like to get it back to him. Looks like a link pulled apart."

"That's odd. Those things are designed to be durable. I haven't sold any since Christmas season and I don't remember engraving the name Caleb on any bracelet. I'll check my sales receipts though." Susan half expected him to bring out a shoebox and weed through them by hand, but no. She was impressed when he pulled up the information on the computer screen.

"Sorry, but I only sold two and they were both women's bracelets."

"Thanks for checking, T.J."

She moved on to the other jewelry store. This one was located in the small mall that went up a few years ago next to the Walmart. The last time she'd been there it'd been packed with holiday shoppers, but on this mid-January morning, it felt like a ghost town. She found the jewelry store, which was one of those national chains. Again she had no luck. *At least my ring got a much needed cleaning,* she thought. She couldn't resist going into the baby boutique and picking up a few outfits for Annalise while she was there. Then she decided to head to the Westbrook Library to look up those other two abduction cases. The librarian knew all the town gossip and had a flawless memory. Maybe she'd shed some light on the case too.

"Good morning, Peggy. I was wondering if I could get any articles you have about those abductions that occurred this past year—the dental hygienist and the bank teller. I'm sure the *Post* gave those stories lots of coverage."

"Sure, Susan. Give me a few minutes. Are you working on a case?"

"I can't give you details, but yes, I am." The librarian rubbed her hands together and went into the back room. *At least some people in town recognize my crime-solving aptitude,* Susan thought.

While she was waiting, Susan drank in the musty smell of old books, the shiny new covers of the recent releases, and the dark wooden shelves—dense with knowledge and history. She'd always loved libraries.

This one was housed in its original building and hadn't undergone any major renovations.

The librarian returned with a small stack of newspapers. Susan sat down at a table and began reading through them. Both of the missing girls had similar physical characteristics, and both had been abducted at their work places. Neither case had been solved. In all likelihood, the same person was responsible for all three disappearances. Did he know his victims, or did he choose them randomly? Did the victims know each other? Susan was determined to find out.

Chapter 7

Jackson and Lynette ushered Sophie's parents into the conference room. Pamela Pearson looked very much like the photos Lynette had seen of Sophie. She was an attractive woman, but as a consequence of recent events, dark circles underscored her eyes and her shoulders drooped as if they supported a bushel full of worries. John Pearson had salt and pepper colored hair and eyes the color of sapphires. He was squeezing his wife's hand.

"We're so sorry you're having to go through this," said Lynette. "We're hoping you may be able to give us some direction. Was Sophie having trouble with anyone? Had she seemed upset lately?"

"Sophie was just beginning to get herself back together after Adam's death. She has mentioned a few friends. She'd begun to see a man named Mitch a few months ago. Mitch the math teacher—that's how she always referred to him. We met him over the holidays. They seemed like a good couple and she was happier than I'd seen her in a long time."

"My wife's right. Sophie was happy except for one thing. Someone had been harassing her. She'd received some threatening phone calls and e-mails. She thought it may have been related to Adam's death, even at this point in time. After the accident, there had been rumors that Sophie had caused Adam's death. Idiotic. Sophie wouldn't harm a fly."

"Adam's family turned on Sophie after his death. They swore that he never would have gone to the edge of a waterfall like that. They claimed that he was afraid of heights—had been since he was a little boy," said Mrs. Pearson. "Adam's brother even made a scene at the funeral, accusing Sophie of killing Adam in front of all those people. He was dressed all fancy in his air force outfit…sure wasn't acting as dignified as he looked."

"Is Adam's brother here in town?" asked Jackson.

"No, I think he went back oversees as soon as the funeral was over."

"What motive did people think Sophie had for murdering her new husband?" asked Lynette.

"Life insurance money. How pedestrian is that? Sophie had a good paying job and she was in love with Adam. It's not like he had a million dollar policy or anything."

"Have you kept in touch with them at all?" asked Jackson.

"Not at all," said Mrs. Pearson. "The last time we saw them was at Adam's funeral."

"Where do they live?" asked Lynette.

"They're still here in Westbrook as far as I know," said Mrs. Pearson. "Except for Sophie's brother, like I said. Please find our daughter for us. I'm so worried about her." She took out a tissue and dabbed her eyes.

"We'll do everything we can," said Lynette. "Have you spoken to Mitch Coniglio?"

"No. We got in late last night and wanted to get here first thing this morning."

"We'll speak to the Bartolo family and to Mitch Coniglio as well," said Lynette. "We tried to question him yesterday, but he was out of town at an educational conference. He should be back today."

"We have a tip line open," added Jackson. "If she was taken against her will, it's likely someone may have heard screaming or witnessed a struggle."

"We're staying at the Rocking Horse Ranch. Please keep us up to date," said Mr. Pearson.

"We will. If you think of anything else, call us," said Lynette. She walked them out of the station. Jackson was already making an itinerary when she came back inside.

"Let's pay a visit to the Bartolos," said Jackson. "After that, we can swing by the school and talk to Mitch, the math teacher."

Just then, Susan walked in. She filled them in on her jewelry store visits.

"Mom, that type of bracelet is so common. I'm not surprised that you didn't learn anything from your visits. And I don't want you going around town asking about the case. It's an ongoing investigation. You could inadvertently be tipping off the bad guy."

"Well, it was worth a shot. You know we have to explore all leads. We don't have much to go on."

"*We?* Stop with that we stuff. This is not your case."

"I mean the police department doesn't have much to go on. I looked up the other two abduction cases. Have you found a connection there?"

Lynette let out a sigh. "Not yet. That trail went cold months ago and so far we have nothing new. But you know I'm not supposed to be discussing this with you."

"I'm just trying to help. I promised Antonio I would."

A distraught blond man pushed open the door to the station. His hair was mussed and he was out of breath. He introduced himself as Mitch Coniglio, Sophie's boyfriend.

"Officer, I just got back into town. My girlfriend, Sophie Bartolo, she's missing. You have to find her. What happened? I knew something was wrong when I couldn't get in touch with Sophie. When I came into school this morning, Mr. Petrocelli filled me in. He told me to come down here right away and talk to you."

"It's detective, not officer, Mr. Coniglio," said Jackson. "When was the last time you had contact with Sophie?"

"Two days ago. I called her from the conference. I was worried about her. She'd been getting threatening e-mails from someone."

"Did she have any idea who was sending them?" asked Jackson.

"She thought it was related to her husband Adam's death. She suspected it may have been Adam's brother. He insisted that Sophie had killed his brother. That was no secret. He was stationed in Germany—he was in the Air Force. She suspected that he'd recently come back into town."

"That's a good starting point. We'll go and speak to him. Call us if you think of anything else," said Lynette. Mitch had calmed down only slightly before leaving the station. Jackson and Lynette pulled up the Bartolos' address and headed out.

Chapter 8

Jackson and Lynette pulled up to a small brick house with white trim. Mrs. Bartolo answered the door. She wore a velour sweat suit and her hair was held in place with a headband. Jackson pulled out his badge.

"Mrs. Bartolo, we're with the Westbrook Police Department. We're working on a missing person case, possibly an abduction, involving your daughter-in-law, Sophie."

"Sophie? She's no longer my daughter-in-law. Missing? Good. Karma is catching up with her..."

"We understand that your family thinks Sophie may have been responsible for your son's death," said Jackson.

"You have that wrong," said Mrs. Bartolo. "We don't think Sophie was responsible for Adam's death. We *know* she was."

"Why do you say that?" asked Lynette.

"Besides the fact that Adam was afraid of heights and never would have gone near the edge of a waterfall, Sophie had a cold, ruthless side to her. When she and Adam were engaged, she was Little Miss Charming. Right after the wedding, she became a first class—let's just say it rhymes with *witch*."

"Can you be more specific?" asked Lynette.

"She started making digs at Adam every chance she got. She was sarcastic and treated him like a worm. Adam even confided in me that Sophie was not the woman he'd fallen in love with. He was beginning to regret marrying her."

"Do you have any idea why her behavior had changed so radically?" asked Lynette.

"And why she wouldn't have just divorced him had she regretted marrying him?" added Jackson.

"She wanted that life insurance money. They were suffering financially. Adam had been laid off at work. His company had been sold and the new owners cleaned house in an effort to save money. Adam and Sophie had bought an expensive home while they were engaged. They couldn't afford to keep it with one income, but with the life insurance money, the whole mortgage could have been paid off. That's exactly what happened. Sophie owns that house free and clear now."

"We read the report and there was no evidence to indicate murder," said Lynette.

"Think about it. A couple goes on a hike, no one else is around. How easy would it have been to push Adam over the edge and claim it was an accident? What evidence could they have? My other son is still pursuing this. He hasn't recovered from Adam's death––not that any of us has. He spends every free minute looking for something to implicate Sophie."

"Have you heard from him recently?" asked Lynette.

"It's been a few days. I've been trying to call since Sophie disappeared, but you know the military. There may be a special training going on where they don't have phone access. Last time we talked, he was flying wounded soldiers out of Iraq and bringing them to the base hospital."

"Could we get your son's name?" asked Jackson.

"Certainly. It's Caleb. Caleb Bartolo."

Chapter 9

Susan couldn't get the name Bartolo out of her head. She was thinking about it all night. Why did it seem so familiar? She hadn't ever met Sophie. She turned on the vacuum cleaner and began going over the living room carpet. Ludwig leaped off the sofa and ran for cover. Susan knew he was going to take refuge under her bed. Johann, on the other hand, remained curled up on the recliner, unruffled by the noise.

Bartolo. Bartolo. Suddenly she remembered. Mike worked with a Scott Bartolo. *I'll bet that's Sophie's father-in-law,* thought Susan. She could stop by to bring Mike some lunch, and who knows? Maybe Mr. Bartolo might just happen to be around. Susan packed a salad into a Tupperware container and grabbed a packet of ranch dressing from the closet. Then she threw together a turkey sandwich. She arrived at Mike's office just as he was about to go on lunch break.

"Hey, Susan. What are you doing here?" asked Mike. He gave her a kiss and smiled.

"Just thought I'd surprise you with some lunch and a hot lunch date."

"I see the lunch, but where's the hot date?" asked Mike. He made a point of turning his head and scanning the office. Susan gave him a playful swat.

"Just kidding," said Mike, rubbing his arm as if Susan had done some damage. "Let's go into the break room." Susan followed him and grabbed a Diet Coke from the vending machine.

"Mike, don't you work with someone named Bartolo?"

"Yeah, Scott Bartolo. He's down the hall from me. Why?"

"I'm wondering if he's any relation to Sophie Bartolo."

"He's her father-in-law. His son's death nearly killed him. I remember how torn up he was after that hiking accident. He was out for months. We were worried that he'd never get over it. I guess you never really recover from the loss of a child, but he pulled himself together enough to come back to work."

"Has he said anything about Sophie being missing? He must be concerned."

"After Adam's death, he was angry at Sophie. Thought she caused Adam's fall."

"Do you think after we finish eating, you could introduce me to Scott Bartolo? Maybe he has some ideas about Sophie's disappearance."

"I can do that, but like I said, there were some hard feelings there. I doubt he's even spoken to Sophie since then."

After they finished eating, Susan followed Mike to an office down the hall. The door was half open, but Mike knocked anyhow. Susan loved that Mike always acted respectful of people's time and territory. He introduced her to a man who looked to be in his early fifties, with neatly cut hair, dressed in khakis and a long sleeved dress shirt.

"Hello, Mr. Bartolo. It's nice to meet you." Susan shook his hand. "Mike has told me so much about you. I'm sure you've heard by now that Sophie Bartolo has gone missing. Her boss, a friend of mine, asked if I would help find her. Do you mind if I ask you a few questions?"

"I don't consider Sophie to be part of my family, not since Adam was murdered. What sort of questions? My wife and I just spoke to the police yesterday."

"Do you know of anyone who may have wanted to harm Sophie?"

"The whole thing has blown over by now, but not for my family. That woman must have had plenty of enemies. She wasn't a nice woman. I could see her rubbing lots of folks the wrong way. Besides, she's a bookkeeper. Lots of folks have bones to pick with bookkeepers."

"I'm so sorry for your loss. I lost my mother last year and I know it doesn't get any easier with time. Thank you, Mr. Bartolo. It was nice meeting you."

"Same here. You can call me Scott."

Susan thought about what Scott had said. It's possible that Sophie's disappearance had nothing to do with her husband's death. Maybe it was related to her position as a bookkeeper. She decided to run over to the school and have a chat with Antonio. As usual, he gave her a magnanimous greeting.

"Susan, so good to see you. What brings you over here? Any news about Sophie?"

"Antonio, I was thinking—did any of your employees handle school funds? Maybe they had some kind of issue with the money that may have caused a rift with the bookkeeper?"

"Not any employees, but now that you mention it, I have a piece of information to share." He closed his office door. "This is totally confidential but I'm telling you this because, first of all, I trust you, and secondly, there may be a connection to the case."

"Go on," said Susan.

"I was transferred here rather abruptly if you remember."

"I do. My friends at the elementary school were sad to see you go."

"It wasn't by choice. The previous principal, Principal Talbot, had gotten into some serious trouble with the law. She was stealing money from the school. Sophie was the one who discovered it. The principal was arrested. She's out on bail awaiting trial and she blames Sophie, of course, for reporting her to the police."

"Would she have been capable of abducting Sophie?"

"I don't think she could have physically done it. Unless she had a gun, maybe. With a weapon, anything is possible."

"Maybe I should pay her a visit."

"Susan, that's ridiculous. It's possible that this woman could have abducted Sophie, with a weapon no less, and you want to go after her? You need to call Lynette. Let the police handle it."

"Why didn't you mention this to the police?"

"Truthfully," replied Antonio, "I didn't think of it until you asked."

"Okay, then. I'll talk to Lynette."

"Good idea. Don't you do anything dangerous."

Chapter 10

Susan got into her car and turned on the radio. She mulled over the new information she'd just learned from Antonio. The former principal of Westbrook Middle was facing jail time for embezzlement and it was Sophie who'd discovered it and turned her in to the police. If that wasn't a motive for hurting Sophie what was? But there was also Caleb, the brother of Sophie's dead husband. Boy was Susan surprised when she found out Caleb was the name of Adam's brother. He'd suspected Sophie of killing his brother Adam and may have recently come back to town after finishing his military service. She'd have to get Lynette to check on that. A third possibility was that it was the work of a seasoned kidnapper. After all, there had been two unsolved kidnappings in the area and both victims bore a physical resemblance to Sophie. Susan was so deep in thought that she nearly ran a stop sign.

Just as she was beginning to feel a migraine starting, the radio broadcast was interrupted with breaking news.

This just in—the missing bank teller who was assumed to have been abducted from the parking lot of Westbrook National Bank six months ago has been found unharmed. The alleged victim reports that she left of her own free will with her ex-boyfriend. Details on the local news at five.

Susan couldn't believe the timing. Just as she'd been considering three possibilities for Sophie's abduction, one had likely been ruled out. Of course, there was still the disappearance in Marlboro—but now that it was no longer linked to the bank teller's abduction, it seemed much less likely that this was a serial kidnapper. Anyway, Susan remembered hearing that in order to be considered a serial crime, there had to be three cases. Her phone vibrated on the seat beside her.

"Hi, Lynette. I just heard the news on the radio that the bank teller was found safe and sound."

"Yes, thank God for that. Anyway, that's why I'm calling. Jason is teaching a class tonight and now that the bank teller has reappeared, I have to stay late at work. Can you babysit Annalise for me?"

"Of course." Susan was always thrilled to spend time with Annalise—especially when Lynette wasn't there to interfere with her spoiling her granddaughter. "Just have Jason drop her off on his way to work."

"Antonio Petrocelli called earlier today. He said he'd spoken to you and remembered that there had been issues between Sophie and the former principal," said Lynette.

"He did. The trial is coming up soon and Sophie was certainly going to be called as a witness, right?" said Susan.

"She was. We'll be speaking to Principal Talbot first thing in the morning."

"And Lynette, one more thing. Can you find out when Caleb Bartolo comes back from military duty?"

"We already did. He has another six months in Germany."

Chapter 11

Susan happily took Annalise from Jason's arms and covered her cheeks with kisses. The little cherub smelled like a fresh spring day. Well, at least when her diaper was clean, she did. At an age where most babies were inclined to cling to their parents, Annalise wrapped her arms around her grandma's neck and let out a squeal. Being a Grandma was more fun than recess.

"I fed her dinner already," said Jason. There's an onesie in the diaper bag, and her bottle is in there too. It should go in the fridge."

"Yes, Jason. I know the routine. I'll have her ready for bed when you come by after class," said Susan. Mike plopped down in his recliner and turned on the TV. Annalise pulled herself up on the coffee table and began exploring the living room on her tip toes. Susan wondered how she'd ever had the energy to chase after Lynette and Evan. A few minutes of running after Annalise and she felt as if she'd just completed a marathon.

"I never get tired of staring at her," said Susan. "She must be the most beautiful baby in the whole world."

"No doubt about that," said Mike. "She acts just like Lynette did at that age—exploring everything. Remember how Lynette used to climb up on the kitchen table?"

"Shhh. Don't give Annalise any ideas."

The TV news flashed a story about the return of the missing bank teller. Mike turned up the volume. "Hey, looks like that bank teller wasn't abducted after all," said Mike. "That's a surprise."

"Yes, I heard it earlier on the radio. After all this time to be found unharmed—her parents must be over the moon about this."

"I know I'd be if it were Lynette or Evan who went missing."

"Now that Sophie's disappearance doesn't seem to be the work of a serial kidnapper," said Susan, "it's possible that Westbrook Middle's former principal could be behind Sophie's disappearance. Do you remember when they arrested her for embezzlement a few months ago?"

"I do," said Mike. "She was a skinny thing; I saw her on the news. I can't imagine that she could have abducted the bookkeeper."

"But if she had a weapon she could have," added Susan.

"I guess it's possible. Seems odd that she'd risk kidnapping charges on top of embezzlement charges, don't you think?"

"She and Caleb Bartolo are the only suspects at the moment. Lynette said Caleb has another six months of military duty over in Germany. He insisted that Sophie killed his brother Adam last year. She and Jackson plan on contacting him."

Annalise tripped over a plastic bowling pin and toppled onto the rug, crying. Mike bought the toy bowling set before Annalise was even crawling in hopes that one day she'd be a bowling buddy. He didn't trust Jason to get his granddaughter into sports. Mike always said Jason was more likely to train Annalise to play the violin or speak Cantonese than do anything physical. Annalise cried. Susan scooped her up and comforted her, then got her dressed for bed. Mike warmed up her bottle in the microwave. As Susan was feeding Annalise, the sight of the bowling pin prompted her to remember that the former principal had been on the same bowling team as one of Susan's former coworkers.

"Mike, can you put the baby to bed after I finish feeding her? I need to go out for a bit."

"Out where?" asked Mike.

Susan decided to opt for a little white lie over starting an argument about snooping. "I was going to do my nails, but I realized I'm all out of nail polish remover. I just need to run over to Rite Aid."

As soon as she was out of the house, Susan scrolled through her phone contacts and found her former coworker's number, immediately hitting the call icon. Fortunately, she answered.

"Hi, Susan. It's been a while since I heard from you. Still enjoying retirement?"

"Sure am. Especially now that I have a granddaughter to dote on. I've also been helping Antonio with a situation at his new school."

"Really? We all miss him over at Westbrook Elementary. Too bad that middle school principal had to turn out to be a thief. That's why they moved him you know."

"So I've heard. Didn't you used to bowl with that principal?" asked Susan.

"She was in our bowling league. Not on my team though. She hasn't shown up since this whole mess began. Word is she only leaves her house once a week to attend Sunday mass. Otherwise, she's become a recluse."

"You know, we have to get together for lunch soon. Maybe on a teacher planning day? I'm flexible—you let me know what works for you."

"Sure thing. I'll see you soon. Enjoy that granddaughter of yours."

Sunday mass, thought Susan. There was only one Catholic Church in town. Susan used to accompany the choir over at St. Augustine's back in the day. They only had two masses on Sundays. *Time to dig out my Sunday clothes thought Susan.*

Chapter 12

On Sunday, Susan showed up at St. Augustine's and planted herself in the last pew. Mike hadn't batted an eye lid when she'd told him that she had to attend church services—to substitute for the sick accompanist. Trying to convince him that confronting a suspected kidnapper and known embezzler was a good plan just would have taken more effort than it was worth. She scanned the congregation and saw many familiar faces, but Principal Talbot wasn't at the early service. She grabbed a donut and coffee in the church lobby after the mass and chatted with various acquaintances while she waited for the 11:00 service to begin. This time, she spotted her target. Principal Talbot came down the center aisle and sat a few rows ahead of Susan. Susan couldn't believe this thief had the nerve to show up at church after breaking one of the Ten Commandments, but hey—who was she to judge? She waited outside the church after the service and made her move when the principal exited.

"Excuse me, but don't I know you? I'm Susan Wiles, retired music teacher from Westbrook Elementary. We brought our chorus to your school every spring for the community sing along."

"Yes, that was a great program. Lots of good publicity for all our schools." Her tone was as flat as a dead man's EKG line. "Excuse me, but I need to be going." She brushed right past Susan.

Susan pretended to walk away, but quietly followed her out to the parking lot and hopped into her Prius. She kept a safe distance between the two cars as she followed Principal Talbot through the center of town, on to a single lane road flanked by apple orchards. A pickup truck entered the road from a roadside fruit stand and gave Susan a buffer between her Prius and the principal's Grand Marquis. When the Grand Marquis turned into a steep driveway, Susan kept going. Then she camouflaged her car behind a patch of trees, parked, and retraced the path up the driveway on foot. Susan regretted having worn pumps, especially given the fact that icy patches shaded by trees still dappled the driveway after the last snowfall. *What was she doing here again, putting herself in the path of a criminal?* She reminded herself that she was looking for a connection between the principal and Sophie's disappearance and swallowed her fear.

The principal climbed up the steps to the front porch and let herself in. Susan took a deep breath and assessed the surroundings. She was standing in front of an old, wooden farmhouse framed by evergreens and bare maple trees. There was a covered, above the ground pool on one side of the house. Also an iron swing set. And an enormous back yard. Susan pulled her scarf more tightly to shield herself from the cold air, and crept around to the back yard. *What do you think you're going to find? Do you think you'll find Sophie out here tied to that red and white doghouse over there?* Susan crept over to the tiny doghouse, expecting to see Sophie tied up and shoved inside with a gag in her mouth, but when she was close enough to peek inside, she could see that neither Sophie nor some Cujo-like guard dog was in there. She looked up at the second story windows, half expecting to see Sophie standing there like Rapunzel awaiting her prince. Nope. Sophie wasn't up there either.

Then she saw it. Outside doors that pulled up and led to a cellar. The house Susan grew up in had had a cellar like that. It had made it easy for her Dad to take tools out to the backyard, but you could also access it through the kitchen via a staircase. Her mom used to store mason jars full of canned tomato sauce and stewed apples down there. This door was closed with a large branch running through the handles. *What a great place to hide a kidnapping victim. And how easy would it be to pull out the branch and do a bit of searching?* She really had no choice but to explore this possibility.

Susan carefully tugged one end of the branch. After a bit of maneuvering, she worked it through the handles and at that moment the door was free. Susan took another deep breath, drank in the smell of the backyard evergreens, and hesitated. *Come on now, Susan. You've got this. There are no monsters in that basement; remember, you came to find Sophie.* She tugged open one of the double doors. A short wooden ladder led into the musty, cave-like basement. The basement smelled like over ripe fruit. With the door open, Susan could see well enough to work her way down the rungs. One rung creaked beneath her shoe. She froze for a moment, held her breath until she was convinced that she was still alone. Then another step. Soon she was standing on a concrete floor. There were some old tools on a workbench, a pool net, a plastic gasoline can, and some firewood. She jumped when she felt something scurry over her feet. And screamed. *Please God, don't let there be mice down here.*

She waded farther into the basement. *Perhaps Sophie was being kept prisoner in a secret alcove of this tomb.* Her feet were killing her. Her hand reached unsuccessfully into her coat pocket for the security of her phone. *Darn it, Susan. Why did you leave it in the car?* She took another step and then she heard it. The cellar door slammed shut from the outside and Susan was swallowed by blackness.

Chapter 13

"Lynette, your mom should have been home hours ago," said Mike. "She was playing the organ for the choir but the last mass should have been over by noon."

"Don't worry, Dad. Maybe she decided to stop at Walmart, or the mall. She could have run into a friend and got talking. You know how Mom loves to talk."

"She would have called. And her phone keeps going straight to voicemail. I know something's wrong. And I know you know it too." Mike paced back and forth as he spoke.

"Jackson went over to the church and talked to Father Anthony. Father said he saw Mom at both masses, but she wasn't accompanying any choir. She was sitting in the pews just like the rest of the congregation."

"And her car? Was it still in the parking lot?" asked Mike.

"No, the parking lot was empty. Dad, I know you're thinking what I'm thinking. Mom probably went there to get some information about Sophie's disappearance. She just can't resist. Otherwise, why would she lie to you about playing for the services? As a matter of fact, why would she even attend one mass—let alone two? The last time I know of her being in a church was at grandma's funeral. What would she be looking for at the church? Better yet, *who* would she be looking for at the church?"

"No idea. I told her not to get mixed up in this. I warned her to keep away from trouble."

"When has that ever stopped Mom?" asked Lynette. "She's going to get hurt one of these days." She paced back and forth across the carpet just as her father had been doing.

"Every time she starts with this new hobby of hers," said Mike, "I'm afraid she'll wind up dead, just like the victims she's trying to help."

"I think I know who she's looking for," said Lynette. "I'll bet she had a hunch that the former middle school principal would be at church and then she could pump her for information. I told her that Jackson and I'd spoken to her and found nothing suspicious, but I knew Mom wasn't going to leave it alone." Lynette took her cell phone out of her pocket and called Father Anthony. Just as she'd suspected. The principal attended 11:00 mass like clockwork, every Sunday. Lynette tried her best to keep a poker face, which she was usually quite good at, but her father saw right through her expression.

"Lynette, I know you just found out something from that phone call. Tell me. I can see it in your eyes. You're terrified about Mom."

"I think we have a lead. I need to swing by the station and pick up Jackson."

"Not without me you're not."

Chapter 14

Susan felt her heart beating like a metronome set to *presto*. Despite the freezing air, she felt the clamminess of cold perspiration on her brow and in her palms. *How am I ever going to get out of here? Think, Susan, think.* Her eyes were beginning to adjust to the dark, but still she could barely see her hand in front of her face. Afraid of bumping into something, she sat down on the frigid concrete floor and tried to formulate a plan. She'd seen a small window but it was near the ceiling and out of her reach. It certainly wasn't letting any light through, probably because it was caked with dust and dirt. She could try throwing something at it, but it would literally be a shot in the dark. Visions of dying cold and alone in this basement swirled in her head. She crept along the floor, not knowing what she was hoping to find. The dust made her sneeze and she could feel torn nylon from her pantyhose on both of her legs.

Her knees ached as she crept along, until she felt the corner of what was either a washing machine or a dryer. Disappointed that it wasn't a door, she continued. Then bingo—an old fashioned fridge. She'd briefly noticed it when she first scanned the basement. *Please God, let it be plugged in.* The front was one solid piece, she ran her hand up the ceramic door until she felt the metal handle. *Slow down, heart. Breathe through your nose, out through your mouth. One, two, three.* She tugged on the door until it opened and light washed over the room. She felt her whole aching body relax as she was at last able to exhale. She was still in a quagmire, but at least she could see now. She reached again into her coat pocket for her phone, then remembered again that it was in her purse. In the car. Parked down the road under the trees.

Think, Susan, think. She climbed up the steps leading into the house but as suspected, the door was locked. *By now Mike is worried and he would have called Lynette. They're probably on their way.* Susan had enough faith in Lynette to assume she'd somehow made the connection between mass, the former principal, and this address. Meanwhile, she had to see if Sophie was down here—drugged, gagged, or unconscious—because heaven knows she hadn't heard anything but her own voice inside her head. She canvassed the basement, looking for a hidden door, or some other hiding place, but found none. Her stomach was rumbling from hunger since she hadn't eaten anything since breakfast.

She noticed a mound of laundry on the floor and began rummaging through it. After a bit of searching, she found a navy sweatshirt with "Westbrook Wolverines" embroidered on the front. It looked too big for the former principal. It had to belong to Sophie.

Chapter 15

"Hurry, Lynette. I've seen you drive faster than this going to Shop Rite to pick up milk. Mom's life is at stake," said Mike.

"Dad, I'm going as fast as I can. You know I want to find her too." Lynette leaned on the gas pedal.

"Turn left here," said Jackson. "The house should be coming up soon."

Lynette slowed down. "Here's the driveway. Look at those tire tracks. They continue and then turn into the bank of trees past the mailbox." There was just enough snow left on the ground to allow the tracks to be visible.

They crawled along in the cruiser until Mike shouted, "That's Mom's car!"

Jackson ran out first, followed by Mike and Lynette. They tugged on the car door but it was locked. Mike kicked the door.

"Wait, I have a key," he said. They saw Susan's purse open on the seat with her phone tucked inside it. "She must be in the house."

The trio made their way to the porch and knocked on the front door. Principal Talbot flung it open from the inside.

Susan heard knocking upstairs. Then she recognized familiar voices. *I knew they'd find me.* Minutes passed like hours. She yelled Mike's name, but doubted he heard her. She screamed for Lynette. *Please don't leave. Come on. Check the basement.*

"Oh, thank God you're here," said Principal Talbot. "There's an intruder in my basement. I caught her snooping around in my back yard and managed to trap her downstairs. I was terrified and I couldn't stop shaking. Thank God you came!"

"Where is she?" demanded Mike. "Where's my wife?" The veins in his neck were bulging.

Principal Talbot pointed to the door leading down into the basement. Lynette insisted on going down first. They ran down the stairs and found Susan holding a sweatshirt in front of a pile of laundry.

"Thank God you're okay," said Mike. He grabbed her and held her tight.

"Thank God *she's* okay? This woman was trespassing in my yard, up to who knows what and you're worried that *she's* okay? I'm pressing charges."

"I hear sirens," said Lynette.

"I called the station three times," said Principal Talbot. "You all sure took your time getting here.

Two officers stormed down the basement steps.

"Ma'am are you okay?" He stood in front of Principal Talbot. "We got a call about an intruder in the house," said one of the officers.

"Thank goodness you came. She's right there," said the principal. She pointed her finger at Susan.

"Officer, we have the situation under control," said Lynette, showing her badge. "Everything is fine here."

The principal threw up her hands and stopped protesting. The two officers left.

"Come on, Mom. Let's get you home," said Lynette.

"That sounds great, but there's something I need to show you first." Susan held up the sweatshirt. "I think I found proof that this woman abducted Sophie."

Chapter 16

A hot shower and take-out pizza had never felt this good. Susan, snuggled into her fluffy bathrobe and pink slippers, relaxed on the sofa next to Mike. *Sixty Minutes* came on television.

"I can't wait till Lynette runs tests on that sweatshirt and proves it belongs to Sophie," said Susan.

"I hope it was worth risking your life over it. You know," said Mike, "It could actually belong to the principal."

"The size was all wrong. Besides, if you'd been recently evicted from your post at Westbrook Middle, would you be waltzing around in one of their sweatshirts? It was in a pile of laundry and must have been worn recently. It has to be Sophie's."

"If they can prove it, maybe they can lean on her and find out where Sophie is. She backed down pretty easily on pressing trespassing charges against you. I'd think it'd be a snap to break her," said Mike.

Susan's eyes were drawn to the TV screen. They were doing a story about adoptees looking for their birth parents. She'd been unsuccessfully hunting for hers for over a year now and any mention of adoption blipped loudly on her personal radar.

"Turn it up, Mike. Those people they're interviewing; they're old—like me."

"Stop it. Sixty-two isn't old."

"No, I don't mean it like that. It's just that most of the time when you hear about adoption stories they feature younger people. I guess by my age you've either found what you were looking for, or have given up. Turn it up."

The story was about a doctor who lived in a small Georgia town back in the fifties. He was no longer alive, but all kinds of evidence had been cropping up implicating him in a baby-selling scheme involving hundreds of children who would now be in their fifties and sixties. According to the story, he was one of a handful of doctors willing to perform abortions as a service to desperate, pregnant women. When these women came to him, however, he managed to talk them into adoption instead, offering to financially support them during their pregnancies, and then place their babies with loving, Christian parents.

"Look, Mike. They're saying this doctor falsified birth certificates and sold the babies to out-of-state couples. Do you think it's possible...?"

"Don't go jumping the gun here. You grew up in New York. How would your parents have even known about this doctor? They lived far from Georgia. And why wouldn't they have gone the traditional route instead of looking at the black market?"

"Maybe they thought this was a traditional adoption. I don't know. My mom was already in her forties when she adopted me. She was probably anxious. Maybe my parents didn't do a whole lot of investigating beforehand."

The reporter was now interviewing an older woman who'd been one of these *Georgia Babes* as they were being referred to. She'd found her birth mother through matching DNA and had formed an organization that traveled throughout the country offering DNA testing to adoptees who've been struggling to find their birth parents.

"Mike, I just remembered something. Mom had an older sister who got married and moved to Georgia. She died when I was still a kid, but I remember Mom mentioning her. It was my Aunt Karen."

"I suppose somehow that could have been a connection but don't you think the odds are slim?"

Sixty Minutes flashed a web address and toll-free phone number to contact for further information. Susan copied down the information.

"Chances may be slim but what do I have to lose? I'm going to find out if they're coming anywhere near here with their testing service. It's just a cheek swab. It's painless and free. Why not?"

"And you're sure you want to know? You keep going back and forth on this."

Susan had certainly been struggling all year with whether or not to search for her birth parents. One day it seemed like a great idea. The next, she was afraid of what she might find. Maybe her mom was in jail or a drug addict. Worse yet, maybe her birth mother simply didn't want her. What if she'd gone to Georgia hoping to get an abortion?

"Mike, I'll always wonder who they are if I don't find them. I'm not good at living with unsolved mysteries, you know that by now."

"Go for it," said Mike. "But know that you're not doing this alone. I'll be right at your side, whatever you decide."

Chapter 17

The next morning, Susan once again questioned the wisdom of searching for her birth parents. A part of her felt as though she was betraying the parents who raised her. Her childhood was rich both in love and in experiences. The loss of her mom last year was still an open wound waiting for a scab to form. On the other hand, what if there was medical history that she should be aware of? And didn't Annalise deserve to know about her true genealogy?

Although her hands were shaking, Susan called the toll free number she'd copied from *Sixty Minutes*. She learned DNA testing was going to be offered in Manhattan in a few weeks. She went ahead and made an appointment, knowing that she could count on Mike to make the trip with her. Blood rushed to her head in excitement as she marked the date on her calendar. She had a feeling this might lead to the answers she'd been seeking.

Meanwhile, it would take at least a few days to get test results back on Sophie's sweatshirt. If the former principal turned out to be innocent, the next most logical suspect would be Adam's brother, Caleb. Caleb thought Sophie had deliberately pushed Adam over the edge of the waterfall to collect the life insurance money. Caleb was still in Germany. He couldn't have abducted Sophie, right?

Susan wondered how plausible it would have been for Sophie to kill Adam. She had benefitted financially from the situation, but why take such a risk? Besides, even if you hated your spouse, it would be quite a leap to commit murder.

Susan dug out the copies of the articles she'd gotten from the library—the accounts of the accident. She needed to see for herself how reasonable it may have been for Sophie to have murdered Caleb's brother.

Maybe Annalise would like a little stroller ride around Lake Minnewaska. Susan knew Jason was at home with her on Mondays and gave him a call.

"Make sure you keep her hat on and the blanket pulled up," said Jason. "I'm not sure Lynette would want her going out in the cold like this."

"You know I'll make sure my grandbaby stays warm," said Susan. "It's a beautiful day and the fresh air will be good for her." Then she took Annalise from Jason's arms and kissed the baby's neck.

"We're gonna have a nice little walk. Right Anabanana?" Annalisa squealed as if she'd understood every word. Susan packed up the stroller and strapped Annalise into her car seat. The sky was as blue as a tropical sea, and as Susan wound her way up the pine-laden mountain, she wondered if she should try painting landscapes. That's a hobby she hadn't tried. What a shame not to capture this scenery.

Lake Minnewaska wasn't far, and since it was a Monday in the middle of January, there were few visitors. She was able to park close to where the trail up the waterfall started. As she pushed the stroller up the hill, she could hear the water spilling down the waterfall. Because it was winter, the trail was closed part way up the mountain, but Susan ducked under the chain, and was able to get to the spot where Adam had fallen. A makeshift wooden cross marker with a rosary around it confirmed she was in the right place.

"Well, Anabanana, there's not even a railing at the edge of the waterfall. And the way this trail winds, it's possible no one would have seen around the bend if Sophie had attempted to push Adam. Someone who's afraid of heights would not have gone all the way to the edge. It is a little creepy looking down at the water here, don't you think?"

"Gaga," said Annalise. That was her name for Susan. Annalise said *Gaga* before she even said *Mama*. Susan took a good look around before heading back to the car. There were many boulders and assorted smaller rocks along the trail. Could Sophie have hit Adam on the head with one of them? Na. That would have left some kind of mark.

"Time to go," said Susan. On the way home, she stopped at the McDonald's with the indoor play area and shared a bit of a vanilla ice cream cone with the baby before dropping her off at Lynette and Jason's. Then she decided to stop by the middle school and have a little talk with the guidance counselor. She wanted to know more about Sophie's character since her curiosity had been piqued. If Caleb was convinced that Sophie murdered Adam, maybe he'd found a way to get back to the states. Perhaps he enlisted the help of a friend. Revenge was a strong motive for wanting Sophie dead.

Susan greeted Antonio and walked back to Elaine's office.

"Hi, Elaine. Are you busy?"

"Not really. What can I do for you? Do you have news about Sophie?"

"Not yet, but we're working on it. You know how you told me there were rumors about Sophie killing her husband?"

"Yes, ridiculous rumors."

"So, there's no way you can imagine anything driving Sophie to that, right? I heard they were having financial issues and the relationship was deteriorating."

"Adam lost his job and they were a bit overextended, so naturally there was tension in the relationship. That doesn't mean Sophie would have killed him."

"What if she'd seen no way out of the financial mess?"

"Susan, you have to keep this confidential, but there was another way." Elaine leaned in closer. "Sophie's old high school boyfriend had come back into the picture. He was her ticket out. The guy owns a plumbing business and Sophie said he wanted her to divorce Adam and he'd take care of her. Sophie was going to do it."

"Elaine, are you sure? Where's this boyfriend now?"

"I am sure, but it doesn't matter. What are we going to say—that Sophie didn't kill Adam because she was going to leave him for an old boyfriend with whom she was having an affair?"

"It would help clear the murder rumors."

"It doesn't matter. There wasn't any evidence that Sophie had hurt Adam, and the rumors have completely died down. What does this have to do with her disappearance? Our focus has to be on finding her."

"Where's the boyfriend now?"

"They called it quits after Adam's death. Sophie was too upset to be involved in a relationship after what happened. She never mentioned him again after Adam died."

Chapter 18

Susan clutched that tantalizing tidbit regarding Sophie and her high school boyfriend firmly in her thoughts. Just because Elaine said he was out of the picture after Adam's death didn't mean it was true. Maybe Sophie had hidden it even from her best friend. She wished she had a name. Perhaps she'd share this news with Lynette. *I think I'll give her a call.* Just at that moment, her phone rang.

"Hi, Lynette. Did you get any results back on the sweatshirt yet?"

"No, Mom. I told you it could take a while. You know, Jason told me you took the baby out in the cold to Lake Minnewaska. What were you thinking? What if you'd fallen or something? No one's around that place in the middle of winter. And Annalise could have gotten sick being out in the freezing air."

"Lynette, calm down. I'd never hurt Annalise. Fresh air is good for babies. She was all bundled up in her hat and snowsuit. I even wrapped two blankets around her. I didn't think you'd mind." Susan sensed an argument brewing.

"You never respect what I say. You only hear what you want to hear." Susan heard Lynette let out a sigh.

"I was just about to call you. I found out something that may possibly help us find Sophie."

"Go on. Tell me the info." Lynette's tone was less angry now that she'd vented.

"I was speaking to Elaine Cummings, Sophie's best friend, and she mentioned Sophie had been seeing her high school sweetheart even though she was married to Adam. Do you think he might be involved in this?"

"Do you have a name? I hope you didn't try to call him or anything stupid like that."

"No. I was hoping you could find that out. Who knows—maybe they even ran away together like what happened with that bank teller everyone thought had been kidnapped."

"She was seeing Mitch Coniglio, remember—Mitch, the math teacher?"

"I know, Lynette. Like I said, maybe it isn't important at all. I thought I'd share it just in case. I was trying to help."

"I'll do a little digging. We don't have much else to go on right now. And next time you think about doing something with Annalise that you know I'd question, how about asking me first?"

"Of course."

Kids can be exasperating. Her mom used to say that all the time. She wondered if her birth mother lacked the patience to raise a child. Maybe that's why she gave her away.

When she got home, Susan decided to check on her adoption web sites before starting dinner. Ludwig snuggled next to her. She hoped she wasn't putting too much optimism into the Georgia Babes possibility, but all the research she'd done about the case since seeing *Sixty Minutes* the other night had made her optimistic that it was at least a possibility. It would be hard to have patience while waiting for the cheek swab appointment. Meanwhile, she continued to explore the old channels as well. There was a woman on one of her chat boards who'd seen the same story and also planned on going for testing. Susan's phone vibrated on the desk.

"Hi, Antonio."

"Hello, Susan. Hope all is well. Have you found out any more information about Sophie? Parents are beginning to ask about her disappearance. It doesn't take long for news to travel these days."

"I found out there was an old boyfriend in the picture back before Sophie's husband died. Elaine Cummings says they'd broken off contact, but Lynette is going to talk to him and see if he has anything to offer."

"Also, Susan, Mitch Coniglio, Sophie's current paramour, dropped by my office today. He said Sophie had mentioned several threatening e-mails and phone calls in the weeks before her disappearance."

"Regarding the embezzlement charges?" asked Susan.

"No. These threats had to do with her dead husband. Someone was taunting her—accusing her of murdering Adam."

"Well, that may be the motive then. Let me share this with Lynette and see what she comes up with."

"Thanks, Susan. Ciao."

While Susan started dinner, she decided to touch base with Lynette once again.

"Hi, Lynette. I have something else to share with you."

"More? You really work fast. I'm still trying to find the name of Sophie's high school sweetheart. I'm going to drop by the Pearsons on my way home and see what they can tell me. Jason already picked up Annalise from daycare."

"Antonio tells me that Mitch Coniglio dropped by his office and mentioned that Sophie was receiving threatening e-mails and phone calls accusing her of murdering Adam."

"Yes, Mitch mentioned that when Jackson and I interviewed him. We're looking into it."

"Of course, he did. Just making sure. I'll see you at Jackson and Theresa's wedding on Sunday, if not before. That's going to be one beautiful wedding. Is your dress ready to go?"

"Yep. Just picked it up from the bridal shop yesterday. Fits like a glove, and isn't bad for a bridesmaid's dress. Jackson is so happy, he's jumping out of his skin. I'm really excited for them both. Of course, it leaves me without a partner for a few days while they honeymoon."

"Well, Lynette, I could kind of stand in for him in an unofficial capacity, of course."

"Oh sure. My mom, the deputy. Run that by Dad, will you? See you Sunday."

Chapter 19

The next morning, Lynette knocked on the Pearsons' heavy oak door.

"Detective, do you have news about Sophie? You found her, right?" said Mrs. Pearson. She was dressed in yoga pants and a long-sleeved tee shirt. Mr. Pearson came into the foyer.

"Did you say you found Sophie?" he said. His eyes were wide with hope.

"No, not yet, I'm sorry to say. I'm just following up on a possible lead. Can you tell me the name of Sophie's high school boyfriend?"

"Her high school boyfriend? You mean Rusty?" said Mrs. Pearson. "She hasn't talked to him in years. Why do you ask?"

"We're just trying to cover all the bases," said Lynette. "If they were still involved, perhaps they had some sort of a fallout and he was reacting to it. Like I said, just trying to cover all possibilities. We don't have much in the way of leads."

Mr. Pearson shrugged his shoulders. "Far as I know, they haven't spoken in years. What about that former principal? She certainly had an ax to grind with our daughter."

"So far nothing, but we're still investigating. Do you know where I might find Rusty?"

"He works with his Dad—family plumbing business. At least, I assume he's still doing that. Worked there all through high school and talked about running it when his dad retired," said Mrs. Pearson. "The shop is down the road from Walmart—Sumter Plumbing. They have quite the monopoly on the plumbing business in this town. They're very good. We've had them out here several times."

"Thanks, Mr. and Mrs. Pearson. I'll keep you posted. We're doing everything we can to find your daughter."

Lynette decided to stop by the plumbing shop. If she hurried, maybe she could catch them before they closed. She pulled up to a gray, cement building which could have been any kind of warehouse except for the old-fashioned water well in front and the billboard with the 't' missing from Sumter. *Sum er Plumbing*, still open. She was greeted by an elderly gentleman sitting at a desk. She assumed he was Mr. Sumter.

"Can I help you?"

"I hope so. I'm detective Green from the Westbrook Police Department. We're investigating a missing person's case. I was wondering if your son Rusty is available to speak with me."

"Missing person? It's that Sophie girl right?"

"You know her?"

"She and Rusty were quite an item all through high school. Can't say I wasn't happy when they broke up though. She was no good for Rusty—always pulling him into trouble. Don't wish bad on nobody though. He's working in the back. I'll get him."

A Ron Howard clone emerged from the back wearing a gray jumpsuit with 'Rusty' embroidered over the front left pocket. Lynette was surprised at how young he appeared. Maybe it was the copper-colored hair and freckles.

"Hello, ma'am. Can I help you?"

"Yes. Let's have a seat. I'm investigating Sophie Bartolo's disappearance. You heard she's missing, right?"

"I heard about her on the news. Made the hair on my arms tingle. I haven't seen her since high school. Sorry I can't be of much help."

"No thoughts on who may have kidnapped her?"

"Nope."

"With all due respect, knock it off, Mr. Sumter. We know you'd been seeing Sophie, even after she married Adam." Lynette's eyes stared through him like a laser.

Rusty squirmed in his seat. "Well, okay. I was seeing her but we'd broken it off after Adam died."

"And you hadn't seen her since? Somehow I'm inclined to think you have. Can't be that close to someone and just end the whole thing and never speak again. Especially not if there hasn't been some huge fall-out."

"We weren't involved like that anymore. We did hang out as friends, but that new math teacher boyfriend of hers is the jealous type. Sophie was afraid he'd lose his cool if he knew she was still talking to me. She was really upset. Someone had been sending her threatening e-mails and voicemails. We thought it was Adam's brother. The guy couldn't let up on thinking Sophie was responsible for his brother's death. I was trying to help Sophie prove that the threats came from him."

"Adam's brother has been stationed in Germany. Sophie knew that. Surely she couldn't have felt threatened by a man stationed across the Atlantic from her?"

"No, no. He's back in town."

"He's not due to come home for another six months. We've confirmed that."

"Well, either the guy has a twin, went AWOL, or he got out early. I saw him at Walmart a few weeks ago. Sophie and I ran into him at Shop Rite late one Saturday night too. He had a few choice words for her right there in the grocery store. Said he hadn't forgotten what she'd done to his brother. Said he had proof that would bring her down."

"Are you sure it was him?"

"I'm a hundred percent positive. Sophie was scared of him. She couldn't sleep that night—called me at two a.m., worried he'd try to break into her house. She thought she heard noises outside."

"Why did she call you and not Mitch?"

"He was out of town. Some kind of convention or conference or something."

"Call me if you remember anything else," said Lynette. She handed him a business card.

"No problem."

Chapter 20

Susan finished her eggs and decided to stop by the station on her way to volunteering at the high school. She thought she'd bring some doughnuts over. Lynette had been working late into the evenings this week, and she said Jackson was running around like a chicken without a head due to his upcoming wedding. *Sugar,* thought Susan. *Yep, sugar was just what Jackson needed.* Maybe he'd chomp down half a dozen Krispy Kremes, then crash and be able to relax. Yep. That was a great plan. Dr. Oz would love that one.

The station was unusually quiet, and Susan couldn't help overhearing a conversation between Jackson and Lynette. After all, the door was wide open. Susan waited behind it for a bit before announcing her presence.

"Jackson, I just got off the phone with my military contact. Caleb Bartolo was discharged from the Air force a month ago due to medical disability."

"What? Why wouldn't he have told his parents? They still think he's in Germany."

"If I were him and had an ax to grind with Sophie, I wouldn't announce my reappearance either. It's a perfect cover. If he was supposed to be in Germany, he couldn't have kidnapped Sophie. He had an alibi."

"What was the medical disability? Did he get shot or something? Post-Traumatic Stress Disorder?"

"They wouldn't tell me. You know, privacy laws and all that," said Lynette.

"Let's find out where he's staying. Rusty and Sophie ran into him a few times. He has to have a place in town."

"And if he's no longer in the service, he needs a job. We should contact the local pharmacies."

Susan stifled it as long as she could. She held her breath. She held her nose. Then it just came out. A sneeze that could have been heard in Manhattan.

"Mom, what are you doing here? Were you eavesdropping?" said Lynette. Her voice was firm as she stared at her mother, who was wedged between the wall and the door.

"Um, no. I mean, of course not." Susan held up the box of doughnuts. "I… I brought you and Jackson a treat." Susan held out the box. Jackson immediately opened the lid and dove in.

"Thanks, Miss Marple. Delish." He took a gooey bite. With bits of glaze still on his lips, he said, "These are my favorite."

"Yes, mine too," said Susan. "Here, have another one." She pushed the box toward Jackson.

"Mom, stop that. You are not going to worm your way out of this one with a box of Krispy Kremes."

"Lynette, I was just coming by to bring the doughnuts and say hello. I swear. When I heard you and Jackson talking, I got caught up in your conversation. I was there literally a minute before I sneezed and gave myself away."

"That was confidential information. You could ruin our investigation if you go blabbing something you overheard here."

"I'm not going to tell anyone. Besides, if it was so confidential, maybe you should have closed your office door," said Susan. "What would your boss say if he walked in and heard you?" Lynette took a step closer. "Don't you wag your index finger at me," said Susan.

"Now, ladies," said Jackson. "Let's calm down." He stepped in between and pushed them away from each other. With sticky lips, he grabbed another doughnut.

Susan took a deep cleansing breath. "Lynette, I can help. Our neighbor is a realtor—you remember Mrs. Crumpet, right?"

"Mom, don't go fishing around for information." Susan wished Lynette wasn't so high strung. She worried about her health with all the daily stress she dealt with.

Lynette hadn't lost the agitation in her voice. "It's not your job. Jackson and I are going to investigate where Caleb may be living or working. Go and buy some new earrings to go with that dress you bought for Jackson and Theresa's wedding. You said last week you needed to do that."

"Yes, Lynette. Condescending as usual. Jackson, I'll see you at the wedding. Can't wait to see Theresa in her wedding gown."

Chapter 21

Susan would go look for the earrings. *After* she stopped by her neighbor's real estate office.

"Hi, Susan. What brings you down here? Have you and Mike decided to sell that house of yours and buy a cottage up in the Catskills? It's about time that husband of yours retired, isn't it? The two of you could be traveling and enjoying your golden years. I could sell your house in a heartbeat with quite a nice nest egg for you guys, I'm sure."

"Oh, yes," said Susan, in the most aristocratic tone she could muster up. "Of course, that's why I'm here. Cabin in the Catskills? How plebian. I was thinking more along the lines of sailing around the world. Got any yachts?"

The realtor laughed. "If I can't sell your house for you, how can I help you?"

"I'm working on a case."

"I'll bet it involves that missing bookkeeper, right? When I saw that story on the news, I said to myself, *they need to get Susan Wiles working on this.* You've become a local hero with your crime solving, you know."

So much for keeping Sophie's disappearance under wraps. The story was all over the news by the next morning. Local hero? That had a nice ring to it.

"I was wondering if any single gentlemen have been around looking for a place recently."

"Hmm, can't say that's happened. Business has been a little slow. The only customers I've had recently have been couples and families. Are you looking for someone in particular?"

"Sophie Bartolo's brother-in-law, Caleb Bartolo. Word is he recently got back from military duty in Germany."

"Caleb Bartolo. Haven't seen him in years. Not since he and that crazy girlfriend of his came in looking for a place. That was years ago."

"Crazy girlfriend?"

"Yeah. Caleb, he was a really nice guy. Polite, clean cut. That girlfriend of his was really off. Once she showed up for an appointment in her pajama pants. Can you believe it? Like I'd bring her to see a house dressed like that. I don't care if the owners had vacated for a while to let us have a look-see in private; I didn't want the neighbors seeing that."

"Was that the only reason you say she was weird?"

"Oh no. She clung all over Caleb, even in public. Started talking about all the kids they were going to have and how all the women in town would be jealous of her having such a handsome husband. They weren't even engaged as far as I know. Caleb seemed really uncomfortable when she talked like that."

"Did you find them a place?" asked Susan.

"No. Caleb broke up with her and that was the end of that. I think he joined the military soon afterwards."

"Do you know if she's still living in town? What's her name?"

"I remember hearing she was locked up in the psych ward for a while. Word was she tried to slit her wrists when Caleb broke things off. Lost track of whatever happened to her. Her name was something with an L. Lisa, Linda, Lindsay. Lindsay, that's it. Lindsay Bateman."

"You've been a big help. When I talk Mike into retiring, I'll be calling you about that cabin."

"Glad to help. I see you and Mike are still taking your walks together."

"When it's not too terribly cold. Otherwise it's the treadmill." She looked at her watch. "Oops, I better get moving." She took a deep breath and mulled over the new information as soon as she left the office. *This might just be the break they were looking for.*

Chapter 22

Now she would stop at the jewelry store. She'd seen a pretty pair of topaz earrings the last time she was there. They would match beautifully with the dress she bought for Theresa and Jackson's wedding. She walked across the cobblestones and into the store where T.J. and his wife were working with Lite FM playing on the radio.

"What can I do for you, Susan?" asked T.J.

"I saw some topaz earrings here last time when I came in about the ID bracelet. I'm going to a wedding and I think they would be perfect with my dress."

"I think you're talking about these." He reached into the display case and took out a velvet box.

"Those are the ones." She ran her finger over then.

"By the way, did you ever find that Caleb fellow you were asking about?"

"Not yet," said Susan.

T.J.'s wife chimed in, "Caleb? I engraved that name on a bracelet not too long ago."

"But I checked the sales receipts. There were only two bracelets sold and they were both women's names," said T.J.

"The woman who wanted it engraved didn't buy it here. She came in with it and asked if we could do the engraving. It was a slow day so I did it for her right then," said T.J.'s wife.

Susan's heart beat a little faster. "Do you remember her name or what she looked like?"

"I don't think I ever got her name. She paid in cash. She had dark hair, maybe in her mid-thirties. A little stocky, I think—unless it was the coat she was wearing."

"Do you remember anything else about her?"

"She seemed a bit impatient considering I was willing to do the job right on the spot."

"Susan, can I ring these up for you?" asked T.J.

"Absolutely. They're gorgeous."

Susan left the shop convinced this was the crazy girlfriend her neighbor had told her about. Was Lindsay Bateman still living in Westbrook, and if so, where? Then she had a thought. Scott Bartolo, Mike's coworker. Surely he'd have some information about the woman who might have married his son. He should still be at the office. She jumped into her Prius and raced over to City Hall.

"Hi, Mike. I was passing by and thought I'd check in on you—make sure you weren't up to no good with that sexy receptionist out there."

"Phew, good thing we were quick," said Mike. He straightened his tie and feigned zipping up his fly.

"Someone's not getting a home-cooked dinner tonight," said Susan.

"Big loss," said Mike. Susan gave him a playful swat.

"So why are you really here?"

"I need to talk to Scott Bartolo. I found out—I mean *we* found out—as in me and the Westbrook Police Department—that Caleb Bartolo had a fiancée before he joined the air force. She may have some information that could help in our search for Sophie."

"Scott should still be in his office. You remember which one it is?"

"I'll be right back." Susan went down the hall and knocked on Scott's door.

Scott looked up from his computer. "Hi, Susan. What can I do for you?"

"Scott, I found out that Caleb had a fiancée before he joined the service. I can't go into detail, but she may have some information that could help us find Sophie."

"I can't see the relationship, but I'll be glad to tell you what I know. Caleb went out with her for about a year. They got engaged, thanks to pressure from Lindsay. Broke up, and she went nuts. My two boys sure knew how to pick 'em. Adam with Sophie and Caleb with Lindsay. Two psychos."

"Do you know if she still lives in town?"

"I think she moved back in with her parents after she was released from the hospital. They live over on Orchard Road." The phone on Scott's desk rang. "If you'll excuse me. I need to take this."

Susan ached to run with this new information and she was soon on her way. Adrenaline flowed like the Rio Grande through her body. Lacking a concrete plan, she prayed for divine inspiration to strike her en route. She had neither a house number, nor a photo of Lindsay Bateman, and would have to rely solely on the realtor's description. Susan crept past pine trees and field stone houses, checking the names on the mailboxes that punctuated the driveways. It didn't take long to find the one labeled *Bateman*.

Now what? I can't, or probably shouldn't, do my own stakeout. It's starting to get dark and Mike will be wondering where I am, especially after the incident with Principal Talbot. If I confront Lindsay, what might she do? She'd been described, after all, as crazy. She had even been in a psych ward. Common sense took over and she headed toward home.

Chapter 23

A solid night's sleep infused Susan with courage. The next morning, she cruised by Lindsay Bateman's house once again. *Did she really expect to catch Lindsay leaving the house? If she did, how would she approach her?* She drove through Krispy Kreme for a doughnut and some coffee. *Didn't detectives always take food with them on stakeouts?* She was hoping her recent indulgences wouldn't prevent her from fitting into her new dress. She planned on going right back to her healthy diet. On Monday.

Parked across the street from Lindsay's house, Susan played a few turns of *Words with Friends* on her phone, fiddled with the newspaper crossword puzzle, and started a grocery list. Luck was with her. A woman fitting Lindsay's description came out of the house with a little white Maltese. While Lindsay walked the dog down the street, Susan had only a few minutes to devise a plan. *Creative Muse, please help me out here. Okay, the direct approach it is.* Susan followed Lindsay down the street, knowing she'd run into her on the return trip. Bingo.

"Excuse me, are you Lindsay Bateman?"

"Who wants to know?" said Lindsay, hands on hips. Susan noticed a different boot on each foot. *Who does that?*

"My name is Susan Wiles. I'm trying to find a man, if you can call him that, named Caleb Bartolo. I heard through the grapevine that you two were once close."

"And? What do you want from me?"

"That son-of-a-you–know-what was dating my daughter. He led her on, said they'd get married, buy a house. And you know what? Without a word, abandons her and joins the military. Out of the blue."

"I'm not surprised."

"You know what he does? Guess. Guess what he does?"

"He trashes her on *Facebook*, right?

"What? Not that I know of. No, he sends her a "Dear John" letter. A "Dear John" letter. My baby won't eat anything but Pop-Tarts, can't sleep. She smells like used running shorts. Hasn't showered in days. I'm worried she's going to try to kill herself. Do you know how to get in touch with him?"

"I believe it. He did the same thing to me. And people thought *I* was crazy. I can't help you. The bastard's still in the Air Force. I haven't seen him in years."

"I heard he was back in town. Thought you might know where he's living or working. I'm going to find Caleb Bartolo and make him sorry he ever looked at my daughter."

"Back in town? What? He's back?" Lindsay's voice rose and she tilted her head.

"That's what I heard."

"That's news to me. Big news. I'm not finished with him yet either." Lindsay's face turned red and her eyes narrowed. "I'll hunt him down and wring his neck with my bare hands after what he did to me. And I'll break his ring finger—for your daughter."

"Not if I find him first," said Susan.

Chapter 24

The stone church on Huguenot Street was nestled between two hills. Snow dusted evergreens surrounded the chapel, reflecting droplets of sunlight onto the stained glass windows. Susan bent down and drank in the perfume of the pastel carnations that were attached to the end of the pew. Then she took her seat between Mike and Jason. Already excited about the wedding, she rubbed her palms together as the priest and Jackson entered.

Pachelbel's Canon floated down from the string quartet perched in the balcony. Lynette, in a deep purple gown, glided down the aisle with the other bridesmaids and ushers. The attendants formed a semi-circle in front of the altar. An organist sat down and the traditional wedding march reverberated through the church. The opening chords brought tears to Susan's eyes. The congregation rose to their feet and gazed at the doors. Susan adjusted her bifocals.

"There she is," said Mike.

"How gorgeous she looks," said Susan. Theresa wore a vintage ivory dress with lace sleeves and a cathedral length train. Susan had seen something similar but not nearly as beautiful on *Say Yes to the Dress*. Theresa's hair was in a loose updo. The veil, waist length, was attached to a sparkly tiara. Susan took a tissue out of her beaded purse. She couldn't help thinking of her own wedding and what a wonderful journey had started that day. Mike was her rock, her best friend, her soul mate. She hoped Theresa and Jackson would be as happy.

Theresa had expressed to Susan how touched she was that the same priest who baptized her and gave her first communion would be marrying her. After some readings, hymns, and an exchange of vows, the priest told Jackson he could kiss his new wife.

The guests formed a receiving line outside the church. The sun was strong, making the cold a bit more bearable.

"Congratulations, Mr. and Mrs. Simpson," said Susan. She hugged them both.

"Take good care of her," said Mike. "You know what they say. A happy wife, a happy life."

At the reception, waiters served trays of cheese pastries and other assorted appetizers. Susan knew most of the guests and took the opportunity to show off pictures of Annalise. Mike brought over a glass of white wine and handed it to Susan. He put his hand on her back.

"Lynette's over by the bar. She wants to talk to you," said Mike. Susan excused herself and maneuvered through the mingling guests.

"Mom, I thought I'd let you know that we got back the tests we ran on Principal Talbot's sweatshirt," said Lynette.

"That's great. It belongs to Sophie, right?" Susan nodded her head.

"Nope. It belongs to Principal Talbot. We have nothing linking her to Sophie's disappearance."

"But that's impossible. Why did she trap me in her basement if she didn't have something to hide?"

"If you found a stranger lurking around, sneaking into your house, what would you have done? Her reaction is nothing out of the ordinary. After all, she even called the police and reported a break-in. On top of that, her alibi checked out, when she finally told the truth about where she was that night."

"Where was that?"

"Atlantic City. She took a bus trip, spent the day and evening gambling, and didn't return until the next day, the morning Sophie went missing."

"Why didn't she say that in the first place?"

"She was already facing embezzlement charges. She thought sharing the fact she enjoyed gambling wouldn't help her reputation. The prosecution could have made a case for her embezzling money to pay off gambling debts."

Balancing a martini and mini-stuffed potatoes, a former neighbor approached them. "Susan and Lynette. I haven't seen you in so long. How's everything? Mike doing okay? Evan?"

"Josie Thompson. It's so good to see you."

"You too, Susan. Lynette, I still look at you and see a little blond tomboy with pigtails. You look beautiful in that dress. Susan, are you still teaching?"

"Nope. I retired last year. Just enjoying my knitting and scrapbooking. And, of course, spending time with my grand-daughter. What about you? Have you retired yet or are you still over at Rite Aid?"

"Still working. With my husband gone I'm not in a big hurry to retire. I'm feeling my age though. Thank goodness they hired another pharmacist. I can't stand on my feet all day like I used to."

"Another pharmacist?" said Susan.

"Yeah. A nice young man. A real looker too. Just got out of the service."

"What's his name?" asked Lynette "Anyone I know?"

"It's Caleb. Caleb Bartolo."

Chapter 25

Lynette dropped Annalise at daycare, then raced over to the Rite Aid where Josie Thompson worked. She was anxious get a look at Caleb's employment application. There were few customers in the store.

"Hi, Mrs. Thompson."

"Lynette. I'm surprised to see you again so soon. Beautiful wedding yesterday."

"Yes, it sure was. I came to follow up on something you said at the wedding. You said you had a new employee—Caleb Bartolo."

"That's right. He doesn't come in until later in the afternoon."

"I need his home address. It's related to a case we're working on."

"Sure. I'll be right back." Josie Thompson went to get the employment information. While she was gone, Susan sauntered into the pharmacy.

"Mom. What are you doing here? This is police business."

"I just needed some more Tylenol. My aching back, you know." She rubbed her lower back and slouched forward a bit.

"Right. So you drove across town instead of going to the Rite Aid that's down the block from you."

"Lynette, I just came by to help. With Jackson gone on his honeymoon, I figured you could use an extra hand."

Josie Thompson reappeared with Caleb's address in hand.

"Here you go. Hope this helps you."

"I'll call you later," said Lynette as she walked her mother to the parking lot.

This was too juicy to leave alone. Susan followed Lynette from the main street to a twisty, unpaved road, trying to stay unnoticed by her daughter. Dense evergreens obscured the view, but Susan knew she was entering farm country. During the summer this road hosted tomato stands and open trucks loaded with corn. In the fall, apples and cider. She meandered up the mountain road, never losing sight of her daughter. She passed a *Dead End* sign, then came to a clearing.

Lynette pulled up in front of an old farmhouse framed with bare apple trees. Behind the wooden homestead stood a converted barn. It wasn't uncommon for farmers in Westbrook to earn extra income by renting out rooms. A car was parked outside of the red barn, signaling to Susan that Caleb must still be home.

As Lynette walked up to the barn, Susan noticed a bulge in her daughter's coat pocket. She knew it was Lynette's gun. *Did Lynette think Caleb was dangerous, or was it just a precaution?* Lynette knocked on the door, but no one answered. She circled the barn, feeling along window ledges and looking under rocks. No key under the doormat either. She tugged at the front door causing loose snow to tumble from the roof. Unable to open it, she peeked inside a window. Then she froze. She stood motionless in front of the window then kicked open the front door with her boot and went inside.

Was Lynette in danger, breaking into a kidnapper's home? Should I call for help? Susan swallowed hard and crept up to the open door. Gingerly, she peered inside. Then, she let out a scream fit for a horror movie. How was this possible?

Chapter 26

Lynette spun around. "Mom, why did you follow me? You keep stepping right in the middle of dangerous situations. Go home."

"Lynette, what happened here? Is that Caleb Bartolo? Is he…is he dead?" Susan worked her way into the room and after digesting the scene, she bent down close to the body. The stench was overpowering. This wasn't nearly as gruesome as the body she'd discovered last year which was run over by a bulldozer, but still, she felt her stomach lurch.

"Don't touch anything. This is a crime scene." Lynette covered her mouth and nose with a handkerchief.

Susan shook off the nausea. "It looks like someone hit him over the head. Who did this? Where's the murder weapon? I bet it's still here." Susan regained her equilibrium and began throwing cushions off the sofa. It was here someplace.

"Mom, I said don't touch. Leave the cushions on the couch. You're messing up the crime scene."

"I'm just trying to help. I know my way around a crime scene."

Lynette grabbed her mother's arm. "Just stop. Don't even walk around. Every time you move you're destroying evidence." Lynette grabbed her phone and called for back-up.

"Do you think Sophie is still here? I can check the bedroom."

"No. Mom. What did I just tell you? Wait outside the front door."

"Okay. I'm going."

From the doorway, Susan absorbed the details of the room. Sparsely furnished. A lamp lay on the floor beside the couch, and an open laptop rested on the floor in front of the coffee table. Susan couldn't help herself. While Lynette climbed up to the bedroom/loft, she crept back in and took a closer look at the laptop. It was open to Caleb's mail. Not wanting to destroy finger prints or anything, she used her gloved hand to scroll through. She checked the sent mail and found three separate e-mails which listed *revenge* as the subject. They were all sent to Sophiegirl@yahoo.com. The first one said, *I have the proof to lock you away for the rest of your life.*

"Mom, get away from there!" screamed Lynette. Susan jumped. She was engrossed in reading the mail and hadn't noticed Lynette descending the ladder.

"Lynette, you have to see this. Caleb was threatening Sophie. He has to have her here somewhere. Or maybe she was able to escape. Do you think she killed him?"

"Mom, shut up. I have to think. If she'd escaped, I'm sure she would have come forward by now."

"Maybe she got amnesia and doesn't remember where she lives or who she is."

"You're watching too many soap operas."

"I'll go home, but please, will you let me know what you find?"

"Mom, this is an open investigation and not your business. You don't seem unnerved by seeing the dead body, so I'm confident you'll be able to drive yourself home. And don't blab to anyone about this. Nobody, kapish?"

"My lips are sealed."

Chapter 27

Later that afternoon, with Mitch, the math teacher at their side, the Pearsons gave a televised press conference. The police hadn't yet publicly announced Caleb's death. Susan felt like the cat who'd swallowed the canary, keeping that information to herself. They didn't find Sophie at Caleb's house, so either Caleb was not the abductor, or Sophie had managed to escape. She noticed bags under Mrs. Pearson's eyes, and Mr. Pearson sported a five o'clock shadow. Imagining herself in the Pearsons' shoes, she wished she could find Sophie for them. Mitch looked—distracted. His eyes stared off into the crowd of reporters. It was hard to tell whether he was distraught, or just numb.

Mr. Pearson stepped behind the microphone and held up a photo of Sophie and one of Caleb. "Please, someone out there may have the key to finding our daughter. If you've seen anything out of the ordinary or had any contact with either my daughter or this man, call the Westbrook Police Department."

Mike turned off the television. "You know, they're focusing on Sophie's parents, and I know they're devastated over their daughter's disappearance, but I was in the office when the police came to break the news to Scott that his second son was found murdered."

"Mike, I was thinking about the Bartolos also. So tragic. Now both of their sons are dead. I can't even imagine the pain they must be feeling."

"Already I'm hearing people around the office whispering that Caleb had snuck back into town and he had probably murdered Sophie. If that's true, then where is she? People should mind their own damn business."

"I know. Instead of supporting Scott, they're busy gossiping about something they know nothing about. I'm sure Scott has caught wind of the office chatter. It does *look* bad for Caleb though. If he did abduct Sophie, then where is she? My guess is that she's dead. She would have turned up by now. But that still leaves the question of who killed Caleb?"

Mike shook his head. "I couldn't begin to guess. Not to change the subject, but I was thinking maybe we could spend the night in the city after your cheek swab. I'm taking Friday off. We could go up early, finish the testing, and maybe take in a show Friday night."

"I'd love that," said Susan. Even though she'd decided to go ahead with the testing, she still had moments when she questioned herself. She knew she shouldn't get her hopes up. *If it's meant to be, I'll find some answers.*

After dinner, she couldn't resist checking in with Lynette to see if she'd uncovered anything at the crime scene that she'd be willing to share.

"Mom, we just started this investigation this morning. It's all circumstantial."

"I knew it. What did you find? Chloroform? Duct tape?"

"Mom…"

"Duct tape, right?"

"Having duct tape in your house doesn't prove anything. There are reasons other than being a kidnapper that a person might have duct tape in the house."

"Like what? Taping up ducts? Sure, Lynette. I'll bet you found some rope too."

"Mom…"

"Okay then. Duct tape and rope. Anything else? Just what is the Westbrook Police Department doing to solve this?"

"How dare you."

"I'm sorry, Lynette. I didn't mean that. I know how hard you work."

"Just to reassure you that your tax dollars aren't being wasted, I'll say this much. We got a call on the tip line after the press conference. Probably nothing. That's all the info you're getting."

Chapter 28

Susan woke up early and got ready to go over to Westbrook High. At least on these mornings when she volunteered, she had a reason to get out of bed and get dressed before lunch. She pulled on a crew neck sweater and black pants with an elastic waist. When she got up to the media center, it was empty. *Where did everyone go?* She peeked around the stacks and saw no one. Then she spotted a small group of staff huddled around a TV in the librarian's office.

"Hey, did I miss something?"

"Boy, look at this," said the librarian. She pointed at the screen. "This morning Sophie Bartolo showed up at the Westbrook Police Station."

"Are you serious?"

"Yes. A motorist saw a dazed woman with no coat on walking on the side of the road. Says he nearly ran her over. He picked her up and took her to the Police Station. Look, they're showing her now."

"Thank God," said Susan. "Thank God she's safe and sound. She doesn't even look any worse for the wear." Susan was convinced after finding Caleb that Sophie was dead too. "If she combed her hair, you'd think she just stepped out of her house to run an errand or something." She tried to call Lynette, but the phone went to voicemail.

"Her parents and boyfriend must be saying a huge prayer of thanks right now," said the librarian.

"Did she say anything, like who took her or where she was being held?" said Susan.

"Not yet. They said there will be more on the evening news."

Susan spent a few hours shelving books in the media center, and left around lunch time. Of course, she'd have to drop by the police station and pump Lynette for some information. She figured if she arrived with a cheeseburger and fries in hand, Lynette would be less angry at her for poking her nose into the case. Of course, Susan would get the same meal for herself. Her diet wasn't going very well these days. She'd focus better after her trip. Then she could ditch the elastic waist pants. *Maybe my birth mother had weight issues and that's where I get it from. Maybe it's not my fault at all that I'm overweight. Maybe it's simply genetic.* The mom she grew up with was naturally thin, and growing up, Susan had always wished she'd inherited her body. Now things were making more sense. When she got to the station, she was surprised to run into Lindsay, Caleb's crazy ex-girlfriend.

"Lindsay, why are you here?" asked Susan. She took a step back.

"The police wanted to ask me a few questions about that son of a bitch ex-boyfriend of mine. He was found murdered. They wanted to know if I'd seen him lately. Of course, I said I hadn't."

"Murdered? Someone besides the two of us must have had it in for him. Any ideas who?"

"Nah. It was probably another one of the girls he dated. We both know how he treated his girls. I'm surprised it didn't happen sooner. Could have been having it out with some girl. No one would have heard them screaming at that out of the way farmhouse. I can see someone whacking him over the head in self-defense, or purely for revenge."

"Well, it looks like he got what was coming to him," said Susan.

"You can say that again." She smoothed out her wrinkled pajama pants. "Gotta get going to the AT&T store. I lost my cell phone and I feel naked without it. I've looked everywhere. Might have to buy me that iPhone6."

"Good luck with that. See you around," said Susan. She walked back to Lynette's office. There was a stack of paperwork on her desk.

"Mom, I'm really busy right now."

"I know, but you have to eat. I brought your favorite meal." She dangled the fast food bag in front of Lynette's nose. She loved the smell of greasy French fries and knew they were one of Lynette's weaknesses.

"Five minutes. That's all."

Susan kept her encounter with Lindsay to herself for now. "Did you find out who killed Caleb?"

"Mom, it's not even been a week. It will take time. This isn't *Law and Order*. Murder cases don't get solved in an hour."

"What about Sophie? What do you make of her sudden reappearance?"

"I'm glad she's still alive. When she didn't turn up right away after Caleb's murder I thought we'd be searching for a body. She's going to be on the evening news. She'll share her story with the public then."

"So you won't give me a little hint as to where she was?"

"No. Watch the news."

Susan replayed her conversation with Lindsay all the way home. How did Lindsay know where Caleb was staying? She had to have been there. Did she murder him? Certainly she had plenty of venom stored up against him. And according to her real estate agent /neighbor, Lindsay was crazy.

Chapter 29

"Mike, come on in. They're showing Sophie now," said Susan. Johann was curled up on her lap, purring like a lawnmower. Mike plopped down on the couch.

"Mrs. Bartolo, let me start by saying how glad we are that you're safe. You gave this town quite a scare," said the reporter. "Tell us your story."

"It's a little hard to talk about, but I'll try. I was at work early, before anyone else was in the office. I was sitting at my desk checking e-mails when Caleb Bartolo came storming into my office. I was surprised, and a bit afraid, to see him. He started hurling threats he was going to go to the police with proof that I'd killed his brother. I never would have killed Adam. I loved him. We struggled. He grabbed my wrists really hard and pushed me against the desk. He started throwing things on the floor. Then he picked up the bronze paper weight off of my desk, held it over my head. Then the last thing I remember is seeing it come toward me. When I woke up, I was tied to a bed, with duct tape over my mouth."

"How horrible," said the reporter. "Did he torture you while you were being held captive? I know you were checked over at the hospital and released this afternoon."

"No. He didn't physically harm me, but psychologically it was beyond horrible. Excuse me a minute." She pulled out a tissue and wiped her eyes. "At least he brought me food and water every night. By day, I assume he was at work. I was always tied to the bed with the tape over my mouth so I figured I must have been somewhere near other people and he was afraid I'd scream. Now I know I was at a motel."

"What do you think he was after? There was never a ransom note."

"He wanted me to confess to killing his brother Adam. Even though I was terrified that he was going to kill me, I wasn't going to admit to something I didn't do." She sniffled and again dabbed at her eyes.

"Now, tell us how you managed to escape."

"One night, he didn't come by with my dinner. He didn't show up the next two nights either. I wriggled my hands against the ropes all night long and somehow I managed to loosen up the ropes enough to escape. That's when I ran out into the street and that Good Samaritan picked me up."

"I'm sure your family is thrilled to have you back. Thank you for sharing your story."

Mike clicked off the TV.

"Glad that story had a happy ending. At least for Sophie. Now let's go pack for our outing to the city," said Mike. He gave her a playful swat on her behind.

"She looks awfully good, don't you think? I mean for being tied to a bed and not eating for three days, she's lucky not to be staying at the hospital rather than going home."

"She looks like a strong woman. Anyhow, she's probably still running on adrenaline."

"I guess you're right. Let's pack."

Chapter 30

Susan barely slept. She tried her left side, then the right, but couldn't get comfortable. She kept imagining what her birth mother looked like and ruminated over reasons why her mother didn't keep her. Maybe she'd been a pregnant teenager, unable to care for a child. She could have given her up so her baby could have a better life than she could offer. That would have been a noble thing to do. *Perhaps they had to rip me from her arms. Maybe she wanted to keep me but her parents wouldn't let her.* She pulled up the extra blanket, then kicked it off. Maybe her mother was in fact married and had other children. Maybe she just didn't want to raise another baby. *Was she too selfish to raise a child? Did she really want to meet this woman?* This whole Georgia Babes thing could be a complete red herring. Would she be disappointed if it was, or relieved? She flipped the pillow over. The alarm buzzed. She heard Mike downstairs starting the coffee.

"Should I make us some eggs?" asked Mike.

"I have a better idea. Let's stop for blueberry pancakes. Howard Johnson's is right on the way."

Still full from breakfast, they arrived in Manhattan later in the morning and walked around Rockefeller Center. The Christmas tree was already gone, but they stood and watched skaters before doing some window shopping. Susan drank in the aroma of hot pretzels and chestnuts as they walked by street vendors. Although she was stuffed, she couldn't resist trying one.

"It's almost time for my appointment." said Susan. Her hands trembled and she dropped the hot pretzel she'd just bought. "I was looking forward to eating that."

"I'll buy you another pretzel. Remember that if anything comes of this, you still have the choice not to contact her. Your life has been pretty darn good without her."

"You're right. Maybe I should blow this whole thing off and we can go to Macy's instead."

"It's your call. Your birth mother could have even died years ago. There may be nothing to find."

Susan sighed. "We're here now. Let's head over to the hospital. I'm just ready to get this over with."

At the hospital, they easily found the lab and sat down in the waiting area. There were half a dozen others, all about Susan's age, waiting to be called. Naturally, they were all anxious to share their stories with each other—perfect strangers who shared a unique bond.

"So where are you from?" asked a woman wearing a leather coat. "Wouldn't it be great if we can get some answers out of this? All my life I've wondered about my parents."

"All your life?" said Susan. "I just found out about being adopted last year when my mom, I mean my adoptive mom, died. I felt so betrayed that she'd kept this from me my whole life. It wasn't right for her to hide this from me. Did she think I'd run off and try to live with my birth mother for heaven's sake? My mom was my mom. I wish she had realized that I loved her too much to ever leave her."

"Really? You just found out? That must have been quite a shock. I feel for you. What makes you think your adoption is related to this whole Georgia Babes thing?"

"I saw it on *Sixty Minutes*. I'd been hitting dead ends everywhere and this made sense. Falsified records? And my mom had a sister who lived in Georgia."

"Same here—*Sixty Minutes* I mean. I've been looking for over a decade."

"If we do find relatives, just think how strange it will be to meet them. What if they're horrible people or they didn't want to be found?"

"Then they wouldn't have joined the registry."

The nurse called Susan back.

"Good luck," she said to her new acquaintance. She scribbled down her e-mail address. "Take this and maybe we can stay in contact. Maybe we'll even find out that you and I are sisters. Wouldn't that be funny?"

Susan just wasn't in the mood for funny. She sat down on one of those chairs they use to draw blood, thankful she was just having a painless cheek swab. Still, her knees were shaking. Mike put his hand on her shoulder. The whole procedure took less than five minutes.

"We'll have the results soon and will enter your information into our database. If we get a match, we'll contact you."

"How long will you keep me registered?"

"We'll keep all our participants in our database indefinably. It may take years, but if a match comes forward we'll let you know."

"Come on," said Mike. "Let's go to the hotel and relax for a bit. Are you okay?"

"Yes. I'm relieved that it's done. The dye is cast, as they say."

"I know you. You would have kicked yourself forever if you hadn't taken this opportunity."

"You know me better than I know myself sometimes." She squeezed his hand.

"We'll try that restaurant Carmine's that Scott recommended. Italian food always cheers you up," said Mike.

At the restaurant later that evening, Susan and Mike were seated near the window, where they could watch the hustle and bustle of the city while they ate. The table was covered in white linen, and a candle encased in frosted glass created a relaxing ambiance. Susan looked into Mike's eyes and was overcome with gratitude that he was her life partner. He was a flying buttress, forever supporting her.

"This eggplant parmigiana is out of this world," said Susan.

"So is my lasagna. I'm stuffed." He patted his stomach.

"Me too, but I saw the waitress go by with the dessert tray. It would be a shame to miss out on the tiramisu."

As they ate their desserts and sipped expresso, the man at the next table got up and staggered toward the restroom. His companion jumped up and grabbed his arm but couldn't prevent him from falling onto the floor.

"I'll call 911," said Susan. She reached for her cell phone while Mike jumped up to help. His experience as a volunteer fireman had proven valuable on more than one occasion. He bent over the body. Susan knew he was listening for a breath. The waitress and manager came over immediately.

"Is he choking?" asked the waitress.

"No, no. He'll be okay. Give him a few minutes. This has happened before. I'm his wife. He just started a new medication for his high blood pressure and sometimes he gets dizzy if he stands up too quickly." She helped her husband up into his chair. "He'll be fine. Thanks for your quick action though."

Another waitress came over and handed the man a damp towel for his forehead.

"She handled that like a pro," said Susan. She couldn't help thinking that she wouldn't have handled it so gracefully had it been Mike keeling over on the floor. Even if this wasn't the first time it happened. The thought of it made her shudder.

Chapter 31

A few days later, Susan was reminiscing about that double-sized tub at the hotel as she fought with the broken handle of her own tub. It had been on the verge of breaking for a while, but Susan hadn't gotten around to getting it repaired. Now she had no choice—at least not if she wanted to shower or take a bath. She figured she could fix it if she had a new part, so she headed over to the plumbing business owned by Rusty's family.

When she pulled into the parking lot, Susan saw Lindsay, Caleb's crazy ex-girlfriend. For a moment Susan wondered if she was simply here because she too had a plumbing issue. *No, that would be too much of a coincidence. Something's fishy here.* Heeding her intuition, she decided to watch. Lindsay went into the shop, then came out minutes later with Rusty's arm around her. Rusty pulled out a cigarette and offered one to Lindsay. *I didn't realize they knew each other,* thought Susan. They finished their smoke, then froze right there in front of Lindsay's car and started kissing. *This has to mean something. It can't be a coincidence that Sophie's high school boyfriend and her brother-in-law's crazy ex-girlfriend are involved with each other.*

After Lindsay left, Susan entered the overheated shop. The dry heat gave her a headache.

"May I help you," said Rusty.

"I hope so." She explained her plumbing issue and Rusty quickly found the correct replacement part.

"I should have taken care of this earlier," said Susan.

"This will be an easy fix. Remember, lefty loosey, righty tighty and it'll be a snap to fix. You just saved yourself the cost of a service call."

"That's good news. Lots of good news lately. For example, isn't it wonderful that the kidnapped bookkeeper, Sophie Bartolo, has returned safe and sound?" Susan knew that was an awkward segue, but hoped Rusty didn't notice.

"Yeah, you bet. That creep Caleb Bartolo sure got what was coming to him though."

"No one deserves to be murdered in his own home," said Susan. "I'll bet it was someone he dated—an ex-girlfriend maybe. Most murders are committed by someone the victim knows." Susan stared into Rusty's eyes, but didn't detect a reaction to her statement.

"If he'd gotten a place in town rather than on that desolate farm, maybe things would have turned out differently for him." *So, he and Lindsay both knew where Caleb was living.*

Rusty's father came in from the back carrying a laptop. He slammed it down on the counter. The sound made Susan jump.

"Rusty, something's wrong with this thing. Can you fix it for me? This is no good for my blood pressure. I don't care how many pills I take, this computer is gonna do me in."

"Sure, Dad. Give me a few minutes."

"So you're good with computers?" said Susan. "My son too. Your generation is so much more comfortable with technology than us old timers."

"You can say that again," said Rusty's father. "If it weren't for Rusty, I'd have thrown that thing against the wall and broken it by now. He can do just about anything with computers."

Rusty just shook his head. "Good luck with that tub of yours. Like I said, easy fix. Call the shop if you have any problems."

She got into her car, and saw Lynette and Jackson pull up. *What are they doing here?* Surely the police didn't need them to hunt down a piece for the station toilet. Luckily, she was parked in the side lot and they hadn't noticed her. Getting out of the car, she decided to perch herself under a partially opened window and see what they were up to.

"May I help you?" said Rusty.

"Hope so," said Jackson. He flashed his badge, and Lynette did the same. "We got an anonymous tip that your plumbing van was parked on Orchard Road, outside Caleb Bartolo's place the night he was murdered."

"No, sir. I wasn't nowhere near Orchard Road that night."

"Can you tell us where you were?"

"Bowling at Westbrook Lanes with some buddies." *Sure, I bet you were,* thought Susan. *More likely hanging out with Caleb's crazy ex-girlfriend. Maybe they both killed him.*

"What time did you arrive at the bowling alley and when did you leave?" asked Lynette.

"Got there around 8:00, left around midnight."

"Can anyone verify your alibi?" asked Jackson.

"Sure." He scribbled something on a notepad and shoved it in Jackson's face. Jackson took a step back. "These are the guys I was with. You can check it out."

"We will," said Lynette.

Yes, we will, thought Susan. She wanted to be sure that Jackson and Lynette had a head start, so she stayed crouched under the window for a few more minutes. She wondered if she'd be able to unkink her legs when she tried to stand up. Had she inherited her weak knees from her birth mother? Rusty's voice floated through the window.

"Hey, I need a huge favor," said Rusty. "If two cops come by and ask you if I was bowling with you the night that Caleb guy was murdered, just say yes. Tell your brother to say the same. Thanks man. I owe you one."

Chapter 32

"Too bad your honeymoon was so short," said Lynette. "Looks like you haven't been getting a whole lot of sleep. Hey, turn left here."

"And it's been worth every minute." Jackson grinned. "Theresa can't take a lot of time off from school right now. We're planning a nice long cruise as soon as summer vacation starts."

"Nice. Lucky you. Here we are. It looks like the farmer is home. Let's hope Caleb's landlord saw something that night. He didn't mention seeing anyone when we interviewed him, but you never know."

"Maybe we can jog his memory," said Jackson.

The farmer came to the door dressed in faded jeans and a flannel shirt. He was caressing a mug of coffee with his bony hands.

"Good afternoon. We're sorry to bother you again, but we need to ask you a few more questions," said Lynette.

"Anything I can do to help Westbrook's finest."

"We received an anonymous tip that someone spotted a plumbing van parked outside Caleb Bartolo's the night he was murdered."

"I don't remember seeing a van, but I was in here watching TV all night."

"You didn't hear anything unusual?" said Jackson.

"No. But come to think of it, I saw a plumbing van parked outside a few days before the murder. Funny thing. I figured if Caleb was having a plumbing problem, he woulda called me first."

"Can you remember anything else that you might have forgotten about?" asked Lynette.

"I don't know if this is important, but Caleb had mentioned a few days before he died that he thought someone had tried to break in. I went over and looked at the place with him. There were no broken windows or anything, so I told him everything looked fine to me. Seemed to satisfy him."

"Anything else?" asked Jackson.

"No, I don't think so."

"Give us a call if you think of something," said Lynette. She handed him a card.

Jackson and Lynette got back into the cruiser.

"It's awfully suspicious how a plumbing van happened to be parked at Caleb's just days before Caleb was killed," said Lynette. "I'm anxious to check out Rusty's alibi for the night of the murder."

"The farmer didn't see the van the night of the murder, though."

"He was inside watching TV. Probably fell asleep in his recliner."

"Or something else was going on between them that had nothing to do with the murder. I still think the ex-girlfriend is guilty," said Jackson.

"Seems a bit too flighty to have carried off a murder, but she was pretty pissed off. You know what they say. Hell hath no fury like a woman scorned. I'm not ruling her out."

Chapter 33

Susan had a monster of a headache from the overheated plumbing shop, so on her way home, she pulled into the Rite Aid where Caleb had worked. She always kept Aspirin in her purse, but when she opened the bottle, she discovered it was empty. She saw her old pharmacist/neighbor behind the back counter and decided to pay for it there rather than at the front of the store.

"Susan, how's it going? What can I do for you?"

"I just want to pay for these." Susan rubbed her temples and passed the box over the counter. As she stood there, her eyes wandered over to Caleb's work area. It seemed like his area had been left untouched. A cork board hung over his desk and displayed a photo of some men in uniform, an outdated calendar, and a Christmas card. She stared at the cork board. Something was off. One side was flush with the wall as expected, but the other was pushed slightly forward. She brought it to the pharmacist's attention.

"I'd never noticed that before. I left everything as is." Josie ran her hands over the edge of the board.

Susan reached over and unlocked the counter opening. Once she could reach his desk, she stuck her fingers between the board and the wall, chipping her nail polish in the process. She tugged at the cork board until one of the nails popped out. *Huh?* A manila envelope was tucked in the hiding place.

"What's that?" asked the pharmacist. "I can't believe I didn't notice it before."

"Strange place for an envelope. Unless, of course, you're trying to hide it." Susan opened the envelope and read over the contents. "This looks like a report from some private investigator. Look at the letterhead."

"Why was he hiding that?" said the pharmacist.

Susan flipped the pages and read through it. "This looks like it's about Adam Bartolo's fall at Lake Minnewaska. See the diagram? It shows the trajectory of Adam's fall."

Josie read over her shoulder. "It says based on the position of the body and the distance from the edge, Adam couldn't have been pushed. The conclusion says it was an accident."

"It sure does," said Susan. She pulled a sheet of legal paper out of the envelope. "This is odd." She turned the paper over.

"What? What does it say?"

"It's pretty cryptic. It says *no push/off,* and there's a handwritten diagram showing the waterfall with arrows and a body at the foot of the cliff. "

"I'll call the police," said the pharmacist.

"No, better yet, I'll drop it by the police station and make sure it gets into Lynette's hands. Let's look more closely at his desk." Susan picked up a small notepad which was next to the phone. "This looks like maybe Caleb wrote something and then tore it off. Hand me a pencil." Susan sketched over the paper with the side of the pencil. "Look at this," she said. Her heart was pumping faster.

"It's a name. Dr. Witherspoon."

"Do you know who that is?" asked Susan.

"No. It's not anyone I've ever heard of. Not a doctor that signs any prescriptions I've seen around here."

"It looks like there's a phone number too but I can't make it out," said Susan. "I'll Google him."

"Better yet, I have a directory of all the licensed doctors in the state. Here. Let me look." The pharmacist flipped through the pages and found four different Dr. Witherspoons listed.

"Too bad we don't have a first name." said Susan. "We'll just have to go down the list and try to find out which one Caleb was calling."

"The first one's a pediatrician. The next is a general practitioner. Can't see why he'd want to talk to either of them."

"Hmm, this one is a forensic pathologist." Susan pushed her bifocals up. "That could be it. Maybe Caleb had a question about Adam's murder, even after reading the report."

"I'm sure your daughter will be able to find him."

"Yes, she's a great detective. I'll give her this information also."

Chapter 34

Susan intended to bring this new information right to Lynette, but in the words of the great poet Robert Burns, 'plans oft times go astray.' The hair on the back of her neck prickled. Was she being followed? *It's just your imagination.* Her arms shook on the steering wheel as she noticed a tan Toyota two cars behind her. It turned left when she did, and kept a safe distance behind. She could feel her pulse pounding like a jackhammer on the side of her neck. *This isn't good.* Rusty drove the plumbing van, so she doubted it was him. *What kind of car does Lindsay drive?* Then she made a sharp right and the car did the same. In her rear view mirror, she couldn't clearly see the driver, but he or she was wearing a hat and scarf. Susan raced through a yellow light. The Toyota passed the car in front of it and ran the red. *Bet he isn't expecting to go where I'm heading.* Flooring the gas pedal, Susan pulled up in front of the police station. When her hands stopped shaking, she let go of the steering wheel. The Toyota had zoomed off. She wished she could remember the plate number. She took a slow, deep breath. Her knees were still quivering. When she finally felt her body was back in equilibrium, she got out of the car.

Inside the station, she discovered that Jackson and Lynette were both out on a call. *Now what? She really needed to talk to her.* Susan decided to help Lynette out and drive over to Dr. Witherspoon's office. He was located in the basement of the hospital—next to the morgue. Knowing all about privacy laws, she devised a plan on the way.

"Hello, Dr. Witherspoon. My name is Susan Wiles. I'm taking a college course in forensics and I was wondering if I could ask you a few questions for an assignment I'm doing."

"A college course?"

"It's one of those courses they offer for retirement learning. Great idea, don't you think? We seniors get to register for all kinds of interesting classes. Never stop learning is my motto. Guess that comes from being a teacher all those years."

"I'm really busy, but I was about to take a lunch break." He looked at his watch. "I guess I can spare a few minutes."

Susan pulled a notepad out of her purse and pushed her bifocals into place. "What sorts of things do you do as a forensic pathologist?"

"I'm a consultant for several neighboring police departments. Sometimes I'm hired by private investigators. Mostly I'm asked to determine cause of death."

"You mean you help solve murders?"

"There aren't a whole lot of actual murders in this area. Sometimes a person dies from no obvious cause— like a heart defect or a metabolic disease. I try to figure out why. Helps the families with closure."

"I just read about a murder in the paper the other day. Man's name was Caleb Bartolo. Did you work on him?"

"That's not something I'm free to discuss,"

"Do you ever find cases of poisoning? Blunt force trauma? Accidental falls?"

"Most of the time, they don't need me for that. Poisons show up pretty readily upon autopsy, and blows that are hard enough to cause death can usually be seen with the naked eye." The doctor glanced at his watch. "I need to be going. Hope I've helped some."

"Oh, yes. Thanks so much for your time."

Susan thought she'd try dropping by the station again on her way home. She couldn't stop analyzing the new clues she'd found. Rusty and Lindsay were involved with each other. They both knew where Caleb lived and had reason to want Caleb dead. Rusty was friends with Sophie and felt protective of her. Maybe protective enough to turn up at Caleb's house, thinking he was holding Sophie. When he didn't find Sophie, maybe he got angry and clobbered Caleb over the head. He'd been seen in the area a few days earlier by Caleb's farmer landlord.

Lindsay hated Caleb for breaking off their engagement and had recently found out that he was back in town. Maybe she went after him. Susan could see that she still harbored lots of anger towards him by the passion and venom that came out of her mouth when speaking about him. And she was crazy. She'd heard that more than once.

She shook the snow off of her boots and went into the police station. Now Lynette was back in her office.

"Mom? What are you doing here?" said Lynette.

"I came by to give you some new information. I went to see Josie at Rite Aid, and we discovered that Caleb had hidden an envelope behind the cork board over his desk."

"You went back to Rite Aid? An envelope? We went over Caleb's work space and didn't find anything like that."

"It looked like the board may have just pulled away from the wall recently." She closed her hand to hide her chipped nail. "Anyhow, to make a long story short, it was a report from a private investigation firm." She handed the envelope to Lynette.

"You took this? If there were any fingerprints on the envelope you've already messed those up. Why didn't you just call me to come get it?"

"I was trying to save you some time. Open it."

Lynette pulled the report out. "This shows that Adam Bartolo was not pushed over that waterfall. We already knew that."

"But this proves it. Now we know Sophie for sure didn't push her husband." Susan handed her the paper from the note pad.

"What's this? Playing secret decoder?" said Lynette.

"It came from Caleb's notepad by his phone. I could tell it had recently been written on. Look. It's the name of a doctor."

"So what? Pharmacists deal with doctors all the time."

"But Josie had never seen the name before and she's worked at Rite Aid for a long time. Josie had this directory and…"

"Mom. Don't even tell me you hunted down this doctor. Please don't tell me that."

"He's a forensic pathologist."

Lynette covered her ears. "I don't want to hear it."

"Works over at the hospital—nice young man."

"Great. Don't you think you should have brought that to me too? I'm surprised he'd even talk to you."

"I have my ways. All I found out was if someone is poisoned or hit with a blunt object, cause of death can be determined during a regular old autopsy."

"And you didn't know that from binge watching *Law and Order*?"

Jackson ran into the office holding a cell phone. "Lynette, we did it. We traced…" He stopped short when he saw Susan.

"Well, Mrs. Fletcher, what brings you here today?" He cleared his throat and hid the cell phone behind his back.

"So you traced that cell phone to…" said Susan. She motioned with her hand as if drawing it out of Jackson's mouth.

"Mom, this isn't any of your business."

"What's the big deal? You traced a lost cell phone. Come on, Jackson. Spill it," said Susan. "You know, I just ran into someone who lost a cell phone. Lindsay, Caleb's ex-girlfriend. It's hers isn't it? I see the leopard case on it. She told me that's the kind of case she had." She was bluffing about the leopard case, but it worked.

"But it's *where* we found it. The evidence guys came across it in the items taken from Caleb's house the day his body was found."

"So that proves that Lindsay was there at his house. She must be the killer," said Susan.

"Mom, all it means is she was there at some time— not necessarily the day of the murder."

"People notice their phones are missing rather quickly. Remember that day you left yours on the park bench when we took Annalise to the playground? You noticed it was missing before we even got back to the car. It couldn't have been sitting there for long."

"Mom, if you want to be helpful, how about swinging by the day care and picking up Annalise? It looks like I'll be staying late tonight."

"You know, I wouldn't give up a chance to spend time with her. Alright. But I'm taking her to the toy store on the way home. And stopping for ice cream."

Chapter 36

"There you go, Annalise. We just made a nice bed for your new dolly with Grandma's knitting project. Doll-sized is as big as that blanket was ever going to get." Susan's cell phone rang.

"That's funny, Anabanana. It rang but then someone just hung up." The phone rang again. This time Susan could see that it was Antonio Petrocelli, her principal friend.

"Hi, Antonio. Did you just try to call?"

"Just now."

Susan shrugged. "I bet things are going more smoothly at Westbrook Middle now that Sophie has been found. Have the parents stopped bugging you?"

"Oh yes. The hoopla has completely died down. I did have something I wanted to talk to you about, though. Remember how Sophie's boyfriend, Mitch, was supposed to have been at that conference during the time that Sophie went missing?"

"Yes, I do. He was shocked when he returned to find her missing."

"I know he was, but I needed his conference fee receipt and hotel bill in order to have him reimbursed. The temporary bookkeeper couldn't find anything, so she called the convention center."

"And?"

"And they had no record of a Mitch Coniglio attending the conference. No hotel bill either."

"That's very strange. Why would he have lied about that?" said Susan.

"I was hoping you could find out for me. If anyone finds out one of my employees was partaking in illegal activities under my nose, it's my neck on the line."

Susan copied down the information about the convention and got Mitch's home address from Antonio. She ran through the reasons that Mitch might have lied. Was he somehow involved with Sophie's disappearance? From all accounts, he and Sophie were a happy couple. On the other hand, who knows what goes on behind closed doors?

Did Mitch have another girlfriend that he was keeping secret from Sophie? Maybe he was married and had a whole other life. She had seen that one on *Dateline* more than once. She couldn't think of any other possibilities at the moment. Maybe she should share this tidbit with Lynette.

Mike came through the door. "Hey, who have we got here?" He swept Annalise up off the floor and gave her a kiss. Annalise giggled and tried to pull off his hat.

"Lynette asked me to watch her; she'll be by soon. Annalise and I had a fun trip to the toy store, right Anabanana?"

Mike took off his coat. "Scott Bartolo came back to work this morning. Only stayed half a day. Poor guy, he's heartbroken, losing a second son like that."

"If we lost Lynette or Evan, I don't think I'd ever recover," said Susan. She sat down on the sofa. "Mike, Antonio called before. He found out that Mitch Coniglio, Sophie's boyfriend, wasn't out of town the day Sophie was kidnapped. The conference had no record of him attending."

"That's weird. Why would he lie about that?"

She shared her theories. "He was back at school before Sophie was found or Caleb was murdered."

"If he had a secret girlfriend, he probably would have taken her to the conference with him. That way the school would be footing the bill. That's what I would have done."

Susan gave him a swat.

Lynette knocked on the door. "Here to pick up my special girl," she said. Annalise ran over to her.

"Lynette, I got a call from Antonio this afternoon. Mitch Coniglio never made it to that conference. He's lying about where he was the day Sophie disappeared."

"Hmmm. We took him at his word. How do you know this?"

"Antonio told me. He must be hiding something. If he wasn't at the conference, where was he?"

"Jackson and I will check into it."

Susan's phone rang. Faint breathing crawled through the line, but then—complete silence. Susan felt the hair on her neck tingle.

"Lynette, Lynette."

"What's the matter?"

"This is the second time today that happened. I heard breathing but the caller said nothing. It comes up as a blocked call."

"Maybe it's just some teenagers pulling a prank," said Lynette. "Why are you answering blocked calls anyway? Who does that?" Annalise tried to squirm out of Lynette's arms.

"She's getting fussy. I'm going to take her home and feed her. If you get any more hang-up calls, let me know right away."

Chapter 37

Lynette arrived at work juggling two cups of Starbuck's coffee, and told Jackson about Mitch being a no show at the conference.

"Sounds pretty darn suspicious to me," said Jackson. "Either it's another girlfriend, or he had something to do with Sophie's kidnapping," said Jackson.

"That doesn't make any sense. He and Sophie had a good thing going," said Lynette.

"Sophie's old boyfriend being in the picture may have awoken the green eyed monster."

"Sophie would have recognized her old boyfriend. She says it was Caleb." Lynette's desk phone rang.

"Well?" said Jackson.

"You're not going to believe this. An anonymous caller insists that he saw Sophie eating solo at a restaurant a few miles outside of Westbrook during the time she was supposed to have been kidnapped."

"That sounds fishy. Why didn't he come forward sooner?"

"He says he didn't pay attention to the whole thing until he saw Sophie on the news the other night. That's when the light bulb turned on," said Lynette.

"Eyewitness reports are unreliable. It was probably someone who looked like Sophie."

"You're probably right." Lynette grabbed her coat. "Let's take a ride over to Mitch Coniglio's and see what he has to say about his phantom appearance at that educational conference."

Mitch was getting out of his car, briefcase in hand, when Lynette and Jackson pulled into his driveway.

"Mr. Coniglio, we have a few questions for you," said Jackson.

"Questions?" Mitch's eyebrow raised. "Sure. Come on in. What can I help you with?"

"You stated that you were out of town at the time Sophie Bartolo disappeared. Is that correct?" asked Jackson.

"Yes, that's right."

"We're a little puzzled, because there's no record of you having registered at the conference. The bookkeeper at Westbrook Middle claims you never turned in a receipt for the reimbursement. I know when I lay out my own money for something work-related, I want that money back ASAP. What happened? "

"No record of you registering at the hotel either," said Lynette.

"Well, there must be some mistake. I swear to you I was there."

"Did you have a fight with Sophie Bartolo? Maybe you and Caleb were working together against a common enemy."

"That's ridiculous, "said Mitch. His jaw tightened. "I won't be insulted like that. Next time you need to question me, it will be with my lawyer present."

Lynette felt in her gut that it didn't add up. Why wouldn't Sophie mention it if she suspected Mitch was involved? What motive did he have? There wasn't a hint of another girlfriend.

"You and your lawyer may need to come down to the station."

"Maybe the convention center and hotel lost my registration. It was snowing pretty hard and the electricity went out for a while."

"We'll check the security cameras. Don't go leaving town or anything," said Jackson.

"I love Sophie. Why on earth would I hurt her? You are barking up the wrong tree while the real culprit is still out there."

In the cruiser, Jackson said, "I can't believe he just lied to us."

"I know he's hiding something. It was written all over his face. I don't think he was involved in the kidnapping though. I think it's something else."

"While we're out, let's see if Lindsay Bateman can tell us what her phone was doing at Caleb's house."

Lindsay Bateman answered the door wearing basketball shorts and a tank top. Her hair was snarled and her hands were splattered with what Lynette hoped was melted chocolate.

"Ms. Bateman, my partner and I have a few more questions for you," said Lynette.

"Okay."

"Have you recently lost your cell phone?" asked Jackson.

"Yep, I did. Just got myself a replacement." She wiped her hand on her shorts, pulled her new phone out of her pocket, and pushed it in front of Jackson's face.

"Where do you think you lost the original?" asked Jackson.

"If I knew that it wouldn't still be lost now, would it?"

"Ms. Bateman, have you ever been to the residence of Caleb Bartolo?" said Lynette.

"Caleb Bartolo? Why would I want to go anywhere near that man?"

"You were once close to him, isn't that right?" asked Jackson.

"Ages ago. Haven't seen the creep in years."

"Can you explain why we found your phone in Caleb Bartolo's bedroom?" said Jackson.

"What? No way. I don't even know where he lives. Thought he was still overseas, till he turned up dead, that is."

"How did you feel when you heard he'd been murdered?" said Lynette.

"Didn't shed any tears over it, but I was surprised."

"Where were you the night it happened?" asked Jackson.

"Home, watching TV with my mom. Ask her. She'll be home from work soon. I wasn't anywhere near Caleb, that's for sure."

"We'll talk to your mom," said Lynette. "Meanwhile, stay in town." Lindsay grumbled as she slammed the door shut.

"Well, now what?" said Jackson. We have Mitch lying about the convention, and Lindsay lying about the phone. Might as well interview Pinocchio next."

"What about the anonymous tipster who spotted Sophie at that restaurant during the time she was abducted?" said Lynette. "Let's follow up on that."

"Probably just a crank call. Some folks just love messing with the police—gives them a sense of power," said Jackson.

"Maybe so. We have some time before Lindsay's mother gets home. Let's drive over to that restaurant and see if anyone who works there saw her." Jackson pulled up the address. "It's not far."

The booths at Donna's Diner were nearly empty at this time of day. The hostess approached with menus in hand. "Can I help you?"

Lynette showed her a picture of Sophie.

"I don't remember seeing her," said the hostess. "Try our waitresses. They might remember her." No one did.

"Strike three," said Jackson.
"Game's not over yet."

Chapter 38

Susan had visions of whipping up a gooey, macaroni and cheese casserole for dinner, but instead, she threw some chicken breasts and vegetables into her cart. Dr. Oz would be proud. She was thinking about Lindsay's cell phone. Lindsay had to have been at Caleb's near to the time of the murder. While examining the possibilities, she practically ran into another shopping cart.

"Susan, how's it going?" It was the mother of one of her past chorus students.

"Enjoying retirement, and my granddaughter," said Susan. "How's Kelly doing? She must be, what? A senior already?"

"She's a freshman in college, can you believe it? You know, she joined the glee club. Still loves to sing."

"Tell her I said hello when you talk to her. How are things with you?"

"They've been better. My dad isn't doing so well. He's at the Veteran's Hospital, upstate. Just got back from visiting him. So sad, all those ex-military people. Lots of young men folk too."

"I'm sorry to hear that. You take care now. Hope your dad feels better soon."

Susan continued pushing her grocery cart. As she walked through the aisles, the hair on the back of her neck felt like porcupine needles. Was she being followed? At Shop Rite? *Now that's just absurd. You have to calm down that imagination of yours before you wind up with high blood pressure or something.* She heard a squeaky cart some distance behind her.

As Susan turned a corner, she saw someone in a parka with the hood pulled up rounding the aisle she'd just left. *Who keeps a parka zippered with the hood up when they're inside? It's really warm in here.* She couldn't even determine if it was a man or a woman. When she got to the produce section, she looked in the fruit display mirror and caught another glimpse of the figure. Now she felt more angry than scared and turned around to approach him. She wheeled her cart quickly in his or her direction, but she wasn't quick enough. The figure sped up, and disappeared down another aisle. *I've lost him.* She called Lynette.

"Mom, calm down. Maybe it was just some homeless person trying to get a handout."

"No, Lynette. That was an expensive parka. Too new for some poor homeless person to be wearing. And if he wanted a handout, why would he have run away when he realized I saw him?" Susan picked at her cuticles.

"So who do you think is *stalking* you?" said Lynette.

"I don't know. You're the detective. I got those hang-up calls too. Something is wrong. I feel it in my bones."

"Go home. Lock your car doors."

"Where are you right now?"

"Jackson and I are coming back into town. We were following up on a dead-end lead from the tip line."

"What kind of lead?" Susan figured Lynette might be willing to share a little info given the incident. Whenever Susan was upset, Lynette did her best to distract her with a juicy bit of information or gossip.

"The tipster saw someone who looked like Sophie at a restaurant during the time she was kidnapped, that's all. We drove over to Donna's Diner, but no one there remembered seeing her."

"Well I hope you get a break in solving the case soon. You know, did I tell you that I saw Rusty and Lindsay together on the street the other day?" She preferred to transfer this bit of information without admitting she'd been hiding out at the plumbing shop."

"No. That's interesting though. Two people with ties to Caleb and Sophie, together."

"I'm sure you'll put the pieces together if in fact they fit," said Susan.

"Feeling better, Mom?"

"Yes. I'm going to go home and cook up some dinner. I was probably making a mountain out of a molehill." Susan put the phone back in her purse. *Maybe it was a macaroni and cheese day after all.* On the way home, she starting thinking about the veteran's hospital that Kelly's mother just mentioned. If Caleb had been injured overseas, wouldn't it make sense that he would have spent some time there? And had Jackson and Lynette checked out *all* the employees at Donna's Diner?

Chapter 39

The next morning, Susan took a ride to Westbrook Middle to drop off some sheet music the new chorus teacher had asked to borrow. Although she'd retired, Susan still had Tupperware bins full of music and teaching supplies that she couldn't bring herself to throw away. As long as she was at the school, she went to say hello to Antonio.

"Susan, always a pleasure to see you," said Antonio.

"You too, Antonio. Has everything gotten back to normal around here since the kidnapping was solved?"

"Yes, yes. Old news. Sophie's back at work and rumors have died down. I haven't gotten any more parent calls concerning safety either. You can stop in and say hello to Sophie if you'd like."

"Thanks, I will." Susan remembered how Sophie's office had looked the last time she'd been there—when it was still a crime scene. Now, you'd never know anything happened. Everything was neatly in place. Sophie was at her desk.

"Susan Wiles, I'd been meaning to call you and thank you for helping Antonio try to find me when I was kidnapped. He told me you were a great help."

"I'm not sure about that, but I am happy that it all turned out okay. Last time I was in here, it looked like a war scene. What happened again that morning?"

"I got to work early. I'm at my desk when Caleb comes stomping in, all red-faced. He starts yelling at me about how he has proof I killed his brother and he was going to get me locked away in prison. I felt scared and decided to leave the office, but then Caleb picks up that bronze paper weight over there on the bookshelf, holds it way high, over his head, and the last thing I remember is seeing it come toward me." Sophie mimicked Caleb's actions. "This wasn't the first time he threatened me, you know. I'd been getting e-mails from him, and even letters." She pulled some letters out of her desk drawer and showed them to Susan.

"Oh, my. That was one vengeful man," said Susan.

Just then, Mitch Coniglio walked in. "Hey, Soph, I was wondering if......"

He stopped to acknowledge Susan. "Hey, are those the letters from Caleb Bartolo? Did Sophie show you these?"

"Yes, just now," said Susan.

"That man was dangerous. Thank God Sophie was able to escape from him. Now that he's dead, at least she can rest easy. I was worried about her all the time when he was alive."

Susan jumped when Lynette walked into the office. Lynette was just as surprised to see her.

"Mom, why are you here?"

"Just had to drop something off for the chorus teacher. You?"

Lynette handed Sophie a form to sign. "We needed Sophie to take care of this paperwork." Sophie signed the paper and handed it back to Lynette.

"I'll walk out with you," said Susan.

"Jackson is waiting in the cruiser. I'm off the rest of the day. Wish I had my own car instead of having to go back to the station first."

"I'll drop you off. It's on my way."

"Thanks, Mom," said Lynette.

"You know, I still wonder how Caleb was able to return early from his duty," said Susan.

"It was a medical discharge," said Lynette.

"Medical? Wouldn't he have had to be under a doctor's care if he was injured seriously enough to be sent home?" said Susan.

"I'm pretty sure he was."

"You know, there is a veteran's hospital just a few hours away. Maybe he saw someone there," said Susan.

"Makes sense," said Lynette. "I know the place you're talking about."

"I don't really have plans today and it's early. Maybe we could ride up there and find out more about Caleb. Unless they tell us he was just plain crazy, I don't understand why he would have taken Sophie. You'd think he'd want to relax and enjoy being home."

"It'll have to be an unofficial visit. Call it a hunch, but I think we should go," said Lynette. Susan wasn't sure she'd heard Lynette correctly. Since when did Lynette agree to take her along on a sleuthing expedition? Lynette was more subdued than usual today. She hoped nothing was wrong.

"By the way, have you heard anything more from the cheek swab?" said Lynette.

"Not yet. I keep waiting for a letter or a phone call, but so far, nothing. Lynette, is something wrong? You're not acting like yourself."

"Mom, listen. I don't want to worry you, but…"

"But what?"

"I've been having some problems with my vision."

"What do you mean? What kind of problems?" asked Susan.

"Halos, fuzziness, tunnel vision—especially at night when I'm driving."

"For how long? Why didn't you tell me sooner?"

"It started a few months ago."

"Did you see a doctor?"

"No, I diagnosed myself using Web MD. Of course, I did. I'm not an idiot. Do you think I'd be saying anything if I hadn't?"

"I didn't mean…"

"The doctor says there's two options. It could be a rare genetic condition that comes on at about my age. It reverses itself by the time you hit your forties. The doctor said it tends to skip generations."

"Does Jason know?"

"Of course, he does."

"And if it isn't that genetic thing?" Susan felt her heart race. Lynette was silent.

"Tell me."

"I think we're almost at the Veteran's hospital." They passed a park full of children.

"Aren't those kids supposed to be in school?"

"I'll bet it's an early release day," said Susan. Anyway, stop changing the subject."

"I'll lose my sight. Are you happy now? I said it aloud."

"Come on, Lynette. Isn't there anything they can do?" Susan felt her neck muscles tense.

"No."

"Lynette, I'm so scared. You might go blind?"

"Do I have to spell it out for you? Yes, I'll go blind. I won't be able to work anymore. We can't live on one salary. And I'll miss seeing Annalise grow up. No graduation gown, no wedding dress…nothing."

"I'm going to find my birth parents. Mark my words," said Susan. "We need that medical history. That will help you, right?" She noticed a few tears on Lynette's cheek, which was a rare sight. Lynette was an expert at appearing stoic. "I'm going to find them, even if this Georgia Babes thing turns out to be a bust. There are other things we can do. Maybe we could even go public, plea for my parents to come forward to help you."

"No, Mom. Don't you dare tell anyone about this. I'll lose my job."

"I understand, but we have to do what we have to do," said Susan. "I saw something on *Sixty Minutes* about using stem cells to cure all kinds of diseases. They can do that now you know."

"You can't say anything to anyone outside of our family. Do you understand?' said Lynette. "And using stem cells is a long way off."

"But, Lynette…"

"Just stop it. I shouldn't have even told you."

"I'm just trying to help."

Susan felt nauseous thinking about Lynette losing her sight. She imagined Lynette learning braille and walking with a white cane.

When they got off the Thruway, they drove down a twisty, country road for what seemed like hours. The sky was gray, not snowing, but overcast. It felt like the car was crawling under a heavy quilt of clouds. They pulled up to a brick, two-story building trimmed in white. A large, American flag flew in front. Surrounded by pine trees, this place looked more like a residence than a hospital.

"Okay, Mom. Let me do the talking when we get inside. They won't easily give away information." Susan watched Lynette wipe another tear from her eye with her glove.

The reception area was small, and smelled like raw onions. When they approached the desk, Susan saw that the lone receptionist was munching on a hero sandwich, oil dripping out of the sides of the bread. Susan couldn't help thinking that the portly, middle-aged receptionist should be eating a salad instead. As expected, the receptionist couldn't reveal whether or not Caleb had been a patient there. Susan motioned to Lynette to follow her into the restroom. She had a plan.

"I'm not sure this is going to work," said Lynette.

"Of course, it will. Come on. It's show time." They returned to the reception area.

Susan moaned. "Oh, no, my chest, my chest! My jaw hurts too, and my right arm."

"Mom, Mom, what's the matter?" Lynette put her hands on Susan's shoulders. "Are you okay? Is it your heart?"

"The doctor said these are warning signs." She rubbed her jaw.

Lynette turned to the receptionist. "This is a hospital, right? Get her back to see a doctor. Now," demanded Lynette. "There's a wheelchair right there. I'll help you." The receptionist put down her sandwich and picked up the phone.

"What are you doing?" asked Lynette. "You need to get her back there right now. She could die. We're gonna sue if you don't do something. Go. Now."

The receptionist wheeled Susan through the double doors. She moved as fast as a fly stuck in honey. Luckily, this wasn't a real emergency. Lynette was told she had to wait in the reception area.

Susan clutched her heart. "I'm sweating and I feel shaky. I need a doctor right now. I'm going to pass out, I feel it." The receptionist disappeared behind the doors, wheeling a moaning Susan.

Then, Lynette got to work. She snuck behind the desk and accessed the computer patient files. She drummed her fingers on the desk. *Come on, come on.* There it was. The information she was looking for. Caleb Bartolo *had been* a patient there. She took a picture of the computer screen. Then she waited. Susan, wearing a hospital gown and clutching her clothes, ran back through the double doors.

"I gave them the slip. Did you get it?" she asked.

"Sure did. Now let's get out of here before we get caught," said Lynette. They ran over the dirty snow, back to the car, both breathing heavily. Susan was shivering and fought to keep the back of the gown closed around her tush.

"So, was he a patient here?" said Susan.

"Sure was."

"Psych ward, right?" said Susan.

"Nope."

"What do you mean, nope? You said he was here."

"He wasn't a psych patient; he was an orthopedic patient. He suffered from a badly torn rotator cuff," said Lynette.

"Rotator cuff? Don't baseball pitchers get that?"

"Yep."

"So what does it mean?" said Susan.

"It means he wouldn't have been able to lift his arm over his head. It would have been too painful."

"Then how could he have conked Sophie on the head with that paper weight, drag her to the hotel, and tie her up?"

"He couldn't have," said Lynette.

Chapter 40

Susan couldn't wait to change into comfortable clothes and plop down on the sofa with her laptop and a cup of hot chocolate. What a day. She rubbed her temples, swallowed a couple of Excedrin, and plunged into her own internet research on eye conditions. Searching for a number of hours, she still hadn't found anything more than what Lynette had said. She searched for ophthalmologists, hoping she'd find a doctor with expertise in this area. She even googled stem cells. Of course, if she could find Lynette's biological grandparents, they could tell her if the disease did in fact run in their family. She went back to her adoption sites and message boards once again.

"Susan, I'm home," said Mike.

"Thank goodness. I really need to talk to you about Lynette." Susan proceeded to relay the information Lynette had given her.

Mike shook his head. "That can't be right. Out of the blue she starts having eye problems? She doesn't even wear glasses."

"It has nothing to do with wearing glasses, and both conditions first come out when a person is Lynette's age."

"I don't know how much harder we can search for your birth parents. I feel like we've tried everything. Lynette's a detective. Why can't she find them? Call the Georgia Babes Foundation. Maybe they've found something by now."

"They said they'd contact me if they found a match. Obviously they haven't."

"If it's genetic, does that mean Evan could get it too?" said Mike.

"I don't know. I suppose so," said Susan. She hadn't thought of that. Evan's medical career would be over before it even started.

"We need to research eye doctors and find someone who knows how to treat Lynette."

"I've been searching online and I'm sure Lynette has been doing the same."

"Then we need to look at universities where research about this is being done. Maybe Jason would have contacts since he works at a college," said Mike.

"And I'll give Evan a call. Maybe one of the faculty members there could lead us in the right direction. After all, Washington University is one of the best in the country."

"Good idea. Will Lynette mind us telling her brother?"

"Too bad if she does. If Evan can possibly lead us in the right direction I'm sure not going to keep it from him."

"Agreed," said Mike. "I know you're in no mood to cook tonight and neither am I. Want to go out and grab a bite?" said Mike.

"Yes, and I know just the place," said Susan. She grabbed a newspaper clipping from the desk, and they were on their way. The sun had already set, and snow flurries clung to the windshield.

"Here it is, on the left," said Susan. They pulled up to a long silver trailer.

"What kind of a dump is this? Donna's Diner? Neon sign out front? I was thinking more along the lines of Vinnie's. And this is so far away. There are plenty of good restaurants closer to home."

"Stop your grumbling. I heard they have excellent food here."

Susan and Mike were seated at a booth. The leather squeaked as they scooted in.

"See. The diner is bustling and it's a week night." They ordered bacon cheeseburgers and a platter of fries.

"I'm positive this place hasn't gotten any Michelin stars. Are you going to tell me the real reason we're here?" asked Mike.

"You know me too well," said Susan. "An anonymous tipster called Lynette and said Sophie was eating dinner here during the time she was supposed to have been kidnapped."

"And you're telling me that Lynette didn't bother checking it out. Come on now."

"She did and no one had seen her, but you know these places have shifts and waitresses have days off. I thought as long as we were going out to eat, I might as well kill two birds with one stone. I'm going to ask our waitress right now." Susan pulled out the newspaper clipping with Sophie's picture. Mike grabbed her arm but it was too late.

"Excuse me, but I was wondering if you've ever seen this woman?" said Susan. "We're old friends but I lost contact with her when she moved. Someone said she'd gotten a place out near here."

The waitress examined the clipping. "I recognize her."

"You do?" Susan felt her pulse quicken. Maybe this was the lead she was looking for.

"Yes, it's that woman, the bookkeeper, who went missing. I saw on the news she's safe and sound."

Susan felt her body relax. "I mean, have you seen her in here? Eating dinner maybe?"

"Can't say I have. You can ask the other girls though."

Susan showed the picture to another waitress and the cashier, but neither had seen her. When she asked yet another waitress, she finally got a different answer.

"Hmmm. She was wearing a wool cap with her hair all tucked up inside, and a scarf around her neck, even while she was eating. I'm sure it was her. I saw her twice. Ate by herself both times."

"Can you check the dates for me?" asked Susan.

"She paid cash. I remember because it's so unusual these days. Can't recall specific dates, but it was a few weeks ago."

"Thank you so much," said Susan.

"Good luck. Hope you find your friend," said the waitress.

Chapter 41

Lynette and Jackson slammed the metal door of the interrogation room. The sterile room was colder than an igloo in Antarctica.

"Come on, Mr. Coniglio. We have proof that you weren't at the conference the day Sophie was abducted. In fact, we have cell phone records that place you at the veteran's hospital. What were you doing there and why are you lying to us?" said Lynette.

Lynette had finally received Mitch's phone and credit card records. Now she and Jackson were going to get the truth out of him.

"I, I'm not lying," said Mitch. Jackson pounded his fist on the metal table.

"We know you're lying. Do you want to add perjury charges to whatever else we wind up charging you with?" said Jackson.

"I didn't do anything wrong. I was helping a friend," said Mitch.

"What friend, Mr. Coniglio?" asked Lynette. Mitch squirmed in his seat.

"Okay, I was helping my girlfriend, Sophie Bartolo."

"By lying about your whereabouts the day she was kidnapped?" asked Jackson. "What was your involvement with her abduction? Were you working with Caleb Bartolo?"

"What? No. That's crazy. Sophie was getting threats from Caleb. He even threatened to kill her. Sophie suggested maybe he was staying at the veteran's hospital since he'd come back to the States. She figured maybe he got injured over there. I was just going there to talk to him," said Mitch.

"And did you?" asked Lynette.

"No. Turns out he wasn't there. It was a dead end. Then it started snowing really hard and the roads were bad, so I stayed over at the Super Eight Motel. I didn't know Sophie was missing until I got back into town. She didn't answer her phone all night. I knew something was wrong."

Lynette handed Jackson the credit card report. "Looks like he's telling the truth about the motel."

"Okay, Mr. Coniglio. You're free to go, but don't go far. We may have more questions," said Jackson. He stuck his thumbs through his belt loops, then followed Lynette back to her office.

"Where do we go from here?" asked Jackson.

"We still have Lindsay Bateman's cell phone found at the crime scene. That's a smoking gun."

"But her mom and she confirmed that Lindsay was with her that night."

"Come on. Her mom? How credible of an alibi is that? After all, she wouldn't want to see her daughter get into trouble. Maybe, just maybe, she lied," said Lynette.

"Don't go getting all sarcastic on me," said Jackson. "What's with you these days?"

"None of her neighbors saw her that night. No one could remember whether or not her car was even in the driveway."

Susan burst into Lynette's office. "Lynette, I have some important information for you,"

"Mom, I thought you were volunteering over at the school today?"

"I am, but I had to tell you this first. Dad and I went out to dinner last night. We went to Donna's Diner."

"Donna's Diner? What gives? You heard us talking about the tipster saying he saw Sophie there, right?"

"You caught me. Anyhow, this is important. One of the waitresses did remember seeing Sophie, twice during the time she was missing. She ate dinner there alone and her hair was all tucked into a hat, like she didn't want to be recognized."

"We already interviewed the wait staff. How is it this person didn't come forward earlier?"

"She was out of town visiting her sick mother the day you went to the diner. Here. I have here name and phone number for you." Susan handed Lynette a slip of paper.

"Good work, Mrs. Fletcher," said Jackson.

"Jackson, don't encourage her," said Lynette.

"Lynette, you have to admit that this is good information. Let's go talk to that waitress."

"If this pans out, looks like Sophie has been telling a whopper," said Lynette.

"Maybe it's that Stockholm syndrome. The victim starts trusting the captor. I saw it on *Dateline*."

"Mom...."

"It's possible that Caleb and Sophie weren't enemies after all. Maybe they wanted some private time and Sophie made up the whole story as a cover up," said Jackson. "Maybe she didn't want Mitch Coniglio to know, or she thought it would look bad if she was seen with her dead husband's brother."

"Maybe Mitch found out and was so angry he killed Caleb," said Susan.

"Or the old boyfriend Rusty did it," said Jackson.

Lynette chimed in. "Could even be Lindsay Bateman. We might as well call in the Long Island Medium. Come on with the guessing. We have to rely on the evidence."

"Let's go back and talk to Lindsay, then Rusty," suggested Jackson.

"Good idea," said Susan.

"Mom, you're expected over at the school."

Chapter 42

Susan was surprised to receive a call from Mike in the middle of the work day.

"Hi, Hon. Scott Bartolo just came by my office and asked if you could come by. Something about Caleb's murder. He wants to talk to you."

Susan felt a little like a peacock fanning its feathers. "Sure. Tell him I'll be right there." She practically flew over to Mike's office. Scott was pacing around his office when she arrived.

"Susan, look. I found this in my gym locker." He handed her a manila envelope. Caleb seemed to have had an affinity for manila envelopes. "Didn't make sense for Caleb to keep up a full time gym membership so when he was home, he used my card to work out. He had my locker combination too. I hadn't been there since before Caleb died. I went this morning and found this."

Susan opened the envelope. "It's a lab report." She skimmed through the papers. "This is the name of some type of drug, I presume. Was it something Caleb was taking?"

"No. He didn't take anything regularly as far as I know."

Susan reread the report. "The signature on this is Dr. Witherspoon. He's the forensic pathologist I spoke to."

"Forensic pathologist? That's the first I've heard about using a forensic pathologist. We had reports from the medical examiner for both of the boys. He found nothing unusual in Adam's system, and it was confirmed that Caleb died from blunt force trauma."

"I think Caleb suspected there was more to Adam's death and he went ahead and hired Dr. Witherspoon to give it a more thorough look. I have a friend who's a pharmacist. In fact, she worked with Caleb. I'll ask her what this medication is," said Susan.

"And there's this phone number in here too," said Scott.

Susan examined the paper he handed her. "Did you call the number?"

"No. What was I going to say? I don't know if it means anything at all. I called you because I figured the police would think I was jumping to conclusions."

"I'm going straight to Rite Aid. I'll call you if I find out anything," said Susan.

"Be careful," said Mike. "We know there's a killer still out there and if he thinks you're getting close to the truth...."

"I know, I'll be careful," said Susan. She loved that Mike was so protective of her and didn't want him to worry, but she had to forge ahead. "I have Lynette on speed dial."

Susan drove across town, frustrated by the midday traffic. She drummed her fingers on the steering wheel. *Come on, move.* She hit each of the three separate traffic lights just as they turned red. *Come on, turn green. I need to get to Rite Aid fast.* A dump truck pulled in front of her. She clenched the steering wheel so hard her fingers hurt. When she finally arrived, she ran into the store and found Josie.

"Josie, I need your help." Susan was out of breath.

"What's wrong, Susan?" said Josie.

"This just turned up. It's a lab report that Caleb ordered. Can you tell me what this medication is?" She showed Josie the report.

"Medipress. It's a blood pressure medication."

"Blood pressure? Is it harmful?"

"Not if you have high blood pressure and take the correct dosage. It's fairly common. Look, I'll show you one." Josie went to the shelf and brought over a capsule. She broke it open and poured out a fine powder. "It's by prescription only."

"Is there any reason a healthy young man like Adam Bartolo would have taken this?"

"Not if he didn't have high blood pressure. I'm not supposed to do this, but I'll see if I can still access his prescription records. He came in occasionally. She spent a few minutes searching. "No, he didn't have any daily medications at all on file."

"So, if someone gave him this drug, could it have killed him?" asked Susan.

"Maybe if he took a whole bottle."

"Could someone have slipped it to him say in food or in a drink?" asked Susan.

Josie licked the powder off her finger. "The taste is bitter, but hypothetically, someone could break open a few tablets and mix them into some strong tasting liquid. Fruit juice maybe. To cover the taste of the amount he would have needed to ingest in order for it to be fatal he would have had to drink gallons of the stuff."

"Thanks, Josie. I may be back."

"Anytime I can help I'm happy to," said Josie.

Susan was trying to connect the dots between Adam's death and the blood pressure medicine but she was stumped. Surely if someone wanted to kill him there were more efficient drugs to use. At the stoplight, she tried the phone number on the paper Scott gave her, but there was no answer. As she continued driving, she got that pins and needles sensation in her arms and legs. Was she in some sort of danger? A car was following her. *Again*? She made several turns just to be sure it wasn't her imagination. The other car did the same. She looked at the plate number and tried to memorize it before pulling into a fire station. It was then that the other car took off. This time she got a few numbers and saw that it was a dark blue Honda Civic. Immediately she called Lynette and told her what just happened.

"Are you okay, Mom?"

"Do you believe me now?"

"This is obviously not your imagination. I'll run the numbers you got and see if anything turns up. Go home and rest. Now it's getting dangerous. You should keep your nose out of things before you wind up getting hurt."

Chapter 43

Susan's legs could barely carry her to the front door. She pulled up her comforter and took a long nap with Johann and Ludwig. Cats and her quilt. There was nothing more relaxing. She woke up abruptly to a knock on the door. It was Lynette.

"Mom, I just wanted to let you know that the car that followed you was a rental. We checked Rusty, Mitch, and Lindsay against the rental records and it wasn't one of them."

"You're sure?"

"I'm not some keystone cop," said Lynette. "Of course, I'm sure."

"By the way, I hadn't had a chance to tell you what I just learned from Scott Bartolo. He found some things in the gym locker he shared with Caleb."

"What?"

"There was a lab report saying Adam had a blood pressure medication in his system. There was also a phone number. I've tried to call it but so far, no luck."

"You tried to call it? Haven't you learned your lesson? I'll check out the medication."

"Are you thinking what I'm thinking?"

"That maybe Sophie drugged Adam and that's what Caleb was holding over her head?"

"I already checked with Josie Thompson. The pills have a bitter taste and it would have been hard to disguise the amount needed to kill him in food or a drink."

"I'm going straight over to see Scott Bartolo. I'm surprised he didn't come to the police with this right away."

"By the way, how are you feeling?" asked Susan

"Fine."

After Lynette left, Susan tried again to call the number Scott Bartolo found. A young sounding man answered. Susan explained the situation and he agreed to meet her at the new Starbucks. She told him to look for a blond lady carrying a flowered purse. He found her right away.

"Would you like some coffee?" asked Susan.

"No thanks."

"I know. Their coffee smells so much better than it tastes. Anyhow, like I explained, your number was left by a recent murder victim, Caleb Bartolo. I'm trying to help his father figure out why he had written it down," said Susan.

"Caleb Bartolo, I remember. He was trying to find out about his brother's fall at Lake Minnewaska. A private investigator he hired had somehow traced me back to the scene. I was there the day his brother died, you know."

"Didn't the police question you? I know they talked to anyone who was in the area."

"I had left by the time the guy died, but I did see the couple having a picnic. I'm a photographer. My partner called me over to photograph a deer, so I was halfway down the trail when he fell. I went back to the studio not even realizing what had happened."

"But you remember seeing a couple?" asked Susan.

"I only remember it because I took a picture."

"A picture?" said Susan.

"A couple enjoying a picnic surrounded by beautiful scenery; waterfall in the background.... I was hired by the park to take photos for an upcoming ad campaign.

Thought it would make a good photo for a brochure or something."

"Do you still have the photo?"

"I do."

"Did you see anything else before you left?"

"Like I told Mr. Bartolo, at one point the guy stands up and starts stumbling like he's drunk or something. I thought it was odd because they'd been drinking what looked like lemonade out of a glass carafe. Even saw lemons floating in it with my zoom lens. I couldn't figure out how he would have gotten drunk—and so quickly at that. Anyhow, that's when I got called away."

"You need to go to the police with this. It could be crucial to solving a double homicide," said Susan.

"If you think it means anything, I will. Mr. Bartolo said not to mention it to anyone, but now that he's dead I guess I don't need to keep that promise."

Chapter 44

Lynette and Jackson called Lindsay back to the station. She still insisted she'd never been at Caleb's and had no idea how her phone had gotten into his house. She swore she was at home with her mother the night of the murder.

"If that girl's lying, she's one heck of a good actress," said Jackson. "A little weird, but doesn't strike me as a killer."

"Purple lipstick, flowered flip flops in January? A little weird is an understatement."

"Let's go back to Rusty. We still don't know why his truck was outside Caleb's," said Jackson.

"Alright. He never mentioned being at Caleb's. Maybe we can jog his memory."

When they got to the plumbing shop, Rusty was out on a job. They questioned his father instead.

"Sir, you told us that Rusty was with you the night of the murder. Is that correct?" said Lynette.

"Yep. We were working late, then grabbed a bite to eat at Vinnie's. By the time we were done, it was late. I dropped him off and took the truck home overnight."

"You're saying *you* drove the truck that night. Where was Rusty's car?" asked Lynette.

"In his driveway. He normally drives the truck."

"Then why were *you* driving that night?" Jackson said. "Why didn't he have the truck that night? How was he going to get to work the next morning?"

"He had the truck. He dropped me off." Mr. Sumter nodded his head.

"But you just said you were driving," said Lynette.

"I was. Rusty's car needed new tie rods so it was at the shop." He nodded again.

"Then how did he get to work?" asked Lynette. "He couldn't have driven to the car repair, and then taken the truck to work."

"Stop already," said Rusty's father. His face was red and his sweat trickled down his brow. He covered his ears with his broad hands.

"You seem confused," said Lynette.

"No. I know Rusty was with me that night. I didn't take my pills this morning. I'm feeling cloudy in the head."

"What pills?" asked Jackson.

"My blood pressure pills. I forgot to pick them up at the pharmacy."

"What medication are you on?" asked Lynette.

"Medi something. Medipress."

When they were back in the cruiser, Lynette reminded Jackson that Medipress was the drug found in Adam's pathology report.

"Sure makes Rusty look guilty," said Jackson.

"Yes, but of which murder? Adam died a year ago."

"That father of his is far from what I'd call a reliable source. I say we check out Vinnie's and the car repair shop. I'm willing to bet Rusty's alibi doesn't check out. Maybe he was involved with *both murders.*"

They headed over to Vinnie's, a long established pizza-rant with green walls, and red and white checkered tablecloths—the colors of the Italian flag. The aroma of fresh bread and oregano flooded through the door. A thick haired, middle-aged man was tossing pizza dough behind the counter. He was the owner of the restaurant, but he had a reputation for getting his hands dirty and putting on a show for the customers.

"What can I do for Westbrook's finest? Can I get you a slice?"

"Vinnie, we're checking out an alibi for the night of January 30. Could you go through your credit card receipts and check if Rusty Sumter and his father were here that evening?" said Lynette.

"Sure. Give me a few minutes." He wiped his flour-laden hands on his apron and disappeared behind a curtain.

"My stomach is rumbling. How about we each get a slice to go?" said Jackson.

"You know, you're going to be one of those middle-aged men with a big old pot belly if you keep eating the way you do," said Lynette. "Do you think Theresa will still love you if you're fat?"

"You know you want some too. I've seen you scarf down half a pie in no time flat. You're just lucky you have a high metabolism."

A while later, Vinnie came back out with a printout from the evening of Caleb's murder. "Yes, Rusty did use a credit card that night. Visa. He paid at 6 p.m."

"Six p.m.? Didn't Rusty's father say they were working late, *then* ate dinner?" said Jackson.

"That's what he said." She looked at the receipt. "It looks about right for two people."

"Maybe there were two people, but not necessarily Rusty and his father," said Jackson. "Vinnie, didn't you install security cameras in your parking lot a while ago?"

"Yes we did. You suggested it. Remember? We had a few smash and grabs so we installed cameras."

"Can we look at the security footage?" asked Lynette.

"I'll have to see if we still have it. After a while we reuse the tape. I'll look."

"Let's hope it still exists," said Lynette.

"Come on back to the security closet," said Vinnie. He rummaged through a box of recordings and found what they were looking for.

"Pop it in the machine," said Jackson. Vinnie hit the play button.

"There's the time. 6:15 p.m. And look. There's Rusty opening up the plumbing truck," said Jackson.

"Sure is, but that doesn't look like his father. Not by a longshot," said Lynette.

"Nope. If you ask me, that looks an awful lot like Lindsay Bateman," said Jackson. "Maybe we should go back and talk to her neighbors."

"We already did."

"But we never asked whether or not they'd seen a plumbing truck hanging around."

"Let's go."

Chapter 45

Susan's phone vibrated. She smiled when she heard her son's voice. He had followed up on Susan's request to ask around for recommendations for Lynette and called with the name of one of the faculty members familiar with rare eye conditions.

"Thank you, Evan. I'll call him right away. I knew you'd come through."

"Maybe you should run it by Lynette first," said Evan.

"Of course. While I have you on the phone, I have a question. You took that pharmacology class last year didn't you?"

"I did."

"Do you know what an overdose of the drug Medipress would do to someone?" asked Susan.

"It's a blood pressure medication. Causes syncope."

"In plain English, hot shot."

"Most of those make people dizzy when they stand up too quickly, especially when someone first starts taking it."

Susan thought back to the night at the restaurant in New York when that man at the next table collapsed. His wife said he'd started on a medication and it caused him to get dizzy. If Rusty wanted to get rid of Adam to get Sophie to himself, maybe he stole the pills from his father and slipped them into Adam's lemonade. Or maybe he and Sophie were working together.

"Thanks, Evan. That helps a lot. Study hard. Miss you."

"Miss you too, Mom. Tell Dad I said hello."

Rusty could have killed Adam because he was still in love with his high school sweetheart, Sophie. He had access to his father's blood pressure pills and could have put them in Adam's drink, with or without Sophie's help. Then he could have come to her rescue again and murdered Caleb when Caleb threatened to come forward with the lab report. Maybe Rusty and Sophie worked together to kill one or both of the Bartolo brothers.

Lindsay Bateman. A jealous nut case who seemed angry enough to have killed Caleb for breaking off their engagement. But she had no reason to kill Adam. Lindsay and Rusty were seeing each other. Maybe *they* worked together to kill Caleb. Both had motive. Susan jumped when her phone rang.

"Susan, this is Pat, T.J.'s wife, from the jewelry store."

"Hi, Pat. What can I do for you?" said Susan.

"Remember when you came by the store and asked about that engraved silver bracelet?"

"I do," said Susan. She reminded herself that the woman who had the bracelet engraved fit Lindsay's description. She had thought maybe Lindsay bought it as a gift for Caleb—trying to win him back.

"I saw something on TV this morning. You know that bookkeeper, Sophie Bartolo, the one who was kidnapped?"

"Yes," said Susan. "I know who you mean."

"I hadn't paid too much attention to it, but last night I was watching an interview with Sophie Bartolo—a rerun from when she first came back. I recognized her. She came into the shop that day to get the bracelet engraved."

"What? Are you sure?" asked Susan.

"I'm positive. I even recognized her voice."

"Thank you for letting me know. I really appreciate it," said Susan. *Brunette, slightly plump,* she realized Pat had originally described *either* Lindsay or Sophie. She'd just assumed it was Lindsay. Johann nuzzled against her legs. Susan opened the blinds so he could get a bit of sunlight. She saw the mailman walking away from her box.

"I'll be right back, Johann," said Susan. The wind was biting, especially since she'd run out without her jacket. She shuffled through the ads and bills until she saw the letter from the Georgia Babes Foundation. She froze in her tracks and held her breath. *Maybe this was the answer she'd been searching for.*

Chapter 46

Susan's hands trembled as she held the envelope. She turned it over and stared at the seal. She couldn't do it. Her knees were shaking so much that she had to sit down. She put the envelope on the coffee table and tried to stop shaking. *I'll wait till Mike comes home.* She looked down and noticed the postmark. The letter had been initially delivered to the wrong address and should have arrived a week ago.

Who am I kidding? I've waited long enough. She tore open the envelope and pushed her bifocals into place.

The Georgia Babes Foundation had located a possible relative and wanted to know if she still wanted to go forward with her search. Didn't she? After all, isn't this exactly what she wanted? Then she took a breath. *What if this relative doesn't want anything to do with me? Is it my Mom? My Dad? Some distant cousin?* She felt like Jell-O. Perhaps she was afraid of the finality. At least now she could fantasize her mother had loved her and never would have given her up if she had any other choice. What if she found out she was wrong? Maybe having a baby was just an inconvenience that her birth mother didn't want to deal with. Maybe she had even taken her home for a while and decided she wasn't worth keeping. Did she cry too much? Drink too much Enfamil?

She wanted to call Mike. She knew she could count on Mike to come home and support her in making this decision. No, this was her decision alone to make.

Within the hour she heard his key in the door. She hugged him tightly and spilled the contents of the letter.

"It's what you've hoped for, isn't it? Besides, now we need to do this for Lynette. If we can find out some medical history it could be a game changer," said Mike.

"You're right," said Susan. She picked up her phone and dialed the number.

"Well, are they picking up?" Mike had his ear next to the phone.

"Shhh. No, it's voicemail. The office is closed. I'll have to try first thing in the morning."

"I'm sure we'll both get lots of sleep tonight," said Mike.

"You don't have to be sarcastic."

He knew her like a book. Whenever she had something big on her mind, Susan tossed and turned all night long, making it hard for Mike to get any sleep either. They started discussing the dinner plan but didn't get far. Susan's phone vibrated.

"Hello. Jason, what's wrong? No. Is she okay? Where are you?"

Mike tugged at her arm. "What's wrong? Is it the baby?"

"Jason, we'll meet you at the hospital."

"The hospital?" Mike grabbed their coats. "Where are we going? What happened?"

"It's Lynette. She was in a car accident. They won't say anything over the phone. Jason has no idea how bad it is but they didn't bring her to Westbrook Medical."

"Why not? Where did they take her?"

"They airlifted her to Dansfield. We have to go right now."

"Dansfield Trauma? That's not good," said Mike. He grabbed his keys. "Let's go."

Mike flew like a shooting star through space to get to Dansfield. Deer crossings and fallen rock zones zipped by before they reached the exit for the trauma center. Snowflakes melted on the windshield and a speeding ambulance passed them as they neared the three-story hospital. *Did they bring Lynette in like that? No, that's right. She came in by helicopter.* Susan picked at her cuticles until they bled. She felt like she was choking.

"We're here. Here's the Emergency Room entrance. Come on." Mike slammed the car door and pulled Susan through the double doors and into the waiting area where they found Jason holding a sleeping Annalise.

"Jason, what's going on? How is she?" asked Susan.

Jason's coat was inside out and his cheeks were flushed. "She's in surgery. It's serious. She was bleeding. Something about her arm, too."

"Jason, how did this happen?" asked Mike.

"I don't know. She was on her way home from work and ran a stop light. She crashed into a telephone pole, that's what they told me."

"Susan hugged Jason tightly. I'll take Annalise." Tears spilled from Susan's eyes.

"Sit down with Jason. I've got the baby," said Mike.

"How badly is she hurt? What are they even operating on?" She looked at her sleeping granddaughter. What if Annalise had to grow up without her mother? She felt like throwing up. *Stop Susan, don't go there.* A doctor came in to talk to them.

"She's still in surgery. There was some swelling around the brain, and we're repairing her arm. We don't know the full extent of her head injury."

"Is she going to make it? Tell me she isn't going to die," said Jason.

"Like I said, we don't yet know the full extent of her injuries. She's with our top neurosurgeon. Let's get her through surgery, then we'll know more."

The doctor left and Jason sobbed like Susan had never seen before. She hugged Jason tight, dampening his shirt with tears.

"It'll be okay," said Mike. "You know how stubborn Lynette is—and strong. She'll get through this."

"She has to. I can't take this."

Jason pulled away. "Why can't they just say that she will be okay—that they'll sew her up, she'll rest here a few days, and be good as new?" His cheeks were saturated.

"This is one of the best trauma centers around," said Mike. "And you heard the doctor. Their best surgeon is working on her."

"I don't know how this happened," said Jason. "Lynette is a good driver; she's never even had a fender bender before. And the roads were clear. It wasn't like they were icy or anything." Annalise stirred.

"Do you have food and diapers for the baby?" asked Mike.

"In the trunk. Lynette always keeps a full diaper bag in there just in case of emergencies."

"I'll run out and get it," said Mike. He took Jason's keys and disappeared behind the door.

Susan tried to be strong for Jason, but she felt like a jellyfish trying to act like a shark. The 'what ifs' hit her too, but she kept them stuffed inside. She couldn't imagine losing Lynette, and prayed that the surgeon could fix whatever was wrong. Jackson and Theresa ran into the room.

"How's Lynette?" asked Jackson. He gave her a hug.

"She's in surgery. We just have to wait." She tried to stop her tears, but the dam was broken.

"We got here as fast as we could. Lynette is a good driver. How could she lose control like that?"

"We're here to help with whatever you need," said Theresa. "It's going to be okay. Lynette is a fighter. I figured I could take Annalise home with me. I know you'll be here all night."

"Thanks, Theresa. That would be a huge help. Mike went to get her diaper bag from Jason's car."

"I saw the accident report. It just doesn't make sense," said Jackson. He turned to Theresa. "If you could take Annalise back, I want to stay. She's my partner. I'm not leaving without knowing that she's okay."

"Of course." Theresa took the baby. "Call me."

Mike came back in with the diaper bag.

"I need to call Evan," said Susan. "And Jason needs to eat something.

"I'll call him," said Mike. "I'll go down to the cafeteria and bring up some food. You stay. I've got this."

Susan sat in the plastic chair next to Jason.

"She'll be okay. She's a fighter." Susan didn't know if she was saying that aloud to calm Jason, or to convince herself. Jason grasped her hand.

Mike came in and put his arm around her. "Evan says this is one of the best trauma centers in the country. He says she's in great hands." He was uncharacteristically quiet as they continued waiting. Susan knew he was swallowing his own worries. Jackson sat down next to her.

"Jackson, do you think this has anything to do with Caleb's murder case? Did someone run her off the road?"

"No, that's one of the first things I asked the officer who was at the scene."

"Did she seem like herself when she left the station? Was something on her mind?"

"She had a headache. She's been getting them a lot these days. Other than that, nothing out of the ordinary."

Susan tried to eat, but couldn't. Her stomach was in knots. She paced around the perimeter of the room until Mike put his arm around her and sat her back down. Jason sobbed into his hands. It was hours before the doctor came to talk to them.

"She had a bleed in her brain. For now, she's holding her own. We'll have to wait until she wakes up to know more."

"Will that be soon?" asked Jason.

"It could be soon, or it could be days. Weeks even. The sooner she wakes up, the more likely it is that she hasn't suffered permanent damage."

"Like brain damage?" said Susan. No...she wasn't going to have brain damage. She would wake up and be back to normal in no time. Mike whispered in her ear.

"Do you think this had anything to do with her eye issues? Maybe she couldn't see."

"My God, I bet you're right. Should we tell the doctor?"

"I don't think it matters at the moment, and remember, Lynette didn't want anyone outside the family to know. I think that includes Jackson."

Hours later, they were allowed to see Lynette for a few minutes. Susan was unprepared for the sight of her daughter. Lynette's eyes were swollen and her face was covered in bruises. Her head was wrapped in gauze, and her arm was in a cotton-lined metal splint. She couldn't control her emotions. Tears poured and she could barely breathe.

"All that swelling is probably just from the airbag," said Mike. "It's not as bad as it looks. They have to wait for the swelling in her arm to go down before they can repair it." Susan trusted Mike's assessment because of his prior volunteer fireman experience, but she couldn't say this was comforting. All she knew was that her baby was hurt and lying in a hospital bed.

Chapter 47

They were up all night, waiting for news. Lynette was in ICU and they took turns sitting at her bedside. There had been no change.

"I hate to have to go, but I need to get to the station," said Jackson.

"What about Annalise?" said Jason.

"She's at our house. Theresa took the day off to stay with her."

Susan and Mike went in to see Lynette. Jason hadn't left her side. Susan was exhausted and could barely stand. Her eyes were raw from crying.

"Why don't you grab a nap on the couch in the waiting room," said Mike.

"I can't settle down enough to sleep. Lynette was stable but still critical. *Please, God. Just let her wake up and be her old self.* She called Theresa and was reassured Annalise was doing fine. That would be Lynette's first priority. *When she wakes up she'll be happy that Theresa stepped in and we were able to be with her.* They stayed at the hospital for a second night. Jackson came by at dawn.

"How is she?" asked Jackson.

"No change. I wish she'd wake up," said Susan.

"Hey, Miss Marple. She's a fighter. She just needs to gather her strength and let her body heal." Susan cried. Jackson tried to cheer her up.

"You know, with Lynette out of commission, I could use some help on Caleb's murder case. If you're up to it."

Susan sniffled, then wiped her moist face. "I guess I could help. I'd be helping Lynette by doing that."

"You sure would."

"I got a call from T.J.'s wife. She works at the jewelry store with him." Susan told Jackson about the bracelet.

"That puts a new spin on things. We were leaning toward Rusty as the murderer, but maybe Sophie was also involved. Sounds like she was going to give that bracelet to Caleb, maybe as a peace offering."

"By the way, did a photographer come down to the station yesterday? He was going to talk to you and Lynette. He was at the lake the day Adam died." Susan wiped her nose.

"We questioned everyone who was there. How is that possible?"

"He left before Adam died, but he has a picture."

"Of what?"

"Of the crime scene, before it was a crime scene of course. He said Adam was walking funny, like he was drunk or something."

"Maybe he was," said Jackson.

"I don't think so. The photographer thought they were drinking lemonade."

"Someone drugged Adam. Is that what you're thinking?"

"Rusty's father takes Medipress. It causes dizziness. The forensic pathologist Caleb hired found the drug in Adam's system. Adam didn't have high blood pressure. There's no reason he should have had it in his system."

"Rusty and Sophie had been seeing each other secretly. He may have been jealous and slipped the drugs to Adam hoping he'd get dizzy and fall."

"That's a big gamble. I think Sophie was in on it. Maybe she was supposed to lead Adam to the edge of the waterfall and give him a little push."

"With the life insurance money, they could have lived happily ever after."

"Rusty was going to inherit the business. I don't think money was the motivator. My money's on jealousy." The doctor came out of Lynette's room. "Let's go back in. I hope Lynette is awake."

Lynette looked just like she had earlier. The doctor said there'd been no change in her condition, but it was a good sign she was holding her own. Susan tried speaking to her. She had heard on Dr. Oz that when people are in comas, they can still hear what's being said.

"Lynette, honey, I'm here. So is Jackson. Annalise is with Theresa. Don't you worry about her."

Mike came in carrying three Styrofoam cups of coffee. "Any change?"

"Not yet."

"Lynette, come on. How did you crash like that anyway? Told you I was a better driver. From now on, I'm behind the wheel of the cruiser."

"Jason hasn't left the hospital." Susan leaned in closer to her daughter's ear. "We're all so worried about you. Evan says this is one of the best trauma centers in the country so you're in good hands. We all love you, Lynette."

Jackson squeezed Lynette's hand. "This is a heck of a way to get some time off of work. I'm stress eating my way through every orange snack in the vending machine. If you don't wake up soon I won't fit in the cruiser."

"Do you think she's going to be okay, Jackson?"

"Lynette is as stubborn as a mule. She won't let a little car accident get the best of her. She'll be waking up any time now, you watch."

Mike put his arms around Susan. "Let's go home for a few hours to shower and check on the cats. If, I mean when, she wakes up you have to be rested and strong."

"You'll call if there's any change?"

"Of course I will," said Jackson.

When Susan walked into her house, Ludwig welcomed her with a meow and rubbed against her ankles.

"I tried talking to her but I don't know for sure that she heard me. Poor Jason looks exhausted. Jackson tries to pretend like he's fine but I can see the concern written all over his face. They've been partners a long time now."

"Of course they're worried. We all are. We'll be back in a few hours. Go take a shower." Susan glanced at the coffee table and saw the letter from the Georgia Babes Foundation. She couldn't handle that right now. She wandered into the kitchen for a glass of water.

"Mike, did you crack open the kitchen window?"

"Are you kidding? It's below freezing outside."

"I know I didn't open it."

"Maybe you needed a little fresh air and just forgot to close it."

"Maybe so. I must have had one of those senior moments or something."

Mike and Susan were out of the house as soon as they showered and fed the cats. When they arrived at the trauma center, the nurse informed them Lynette was in stable but critical condition. She hadn't yet woken up.

Susan had to swallow hard to keep from crying when she entered Lynette's room. There were tubes and so many wires. A foreboding hum came from the machines attached to her daughter. She grabbed Mike's hand. She saw frown lines around his eyes and mouth. Then she noticed a large bouquet on the dresser.

Trying to remain positive, she said, "Lynette, these flowers are beautiful." She took a sniff and read the card. "They're from your friends at the station. Isn't that thoughtful?" There was no response. "These are gorgeous too. Carnations last forever. I don't see a card. I wonder who sent them?"

"I'm going to drag Jason down to the cafeteria for some food. He'll be no good to Lynette or Annalise if he makes himself sick," said Mike. He gave Lynette a kiss on the forehead.

"Your Dad is taking care of Jason for you. I got a call from T.J.'s wife, you know, at the jewelry store. She swears it was Sophie who got that bracelet engraved, not Lindsay. They look alike you know."

Lynette began to stir. "Honey, wake up, that's it."

"Mmmm."

"Honey."

"Mom."

"Open your eyes," said Susan.

Lynette groaned. Then she opened her eyes and turned her head. "Mom, where am I?"

"You're at Dansfield Trauma Center. You were in a car accident."

"Car accident? Annalise?"

"She's just fine. We're taking good care of her."

"My head hurts bad."

"Do you remember what happened?"

"What?"

"Do you remember what happened?"

"I think so. I was driving home. It was dark out. I couldn't see."

"Couldn't see?"

"My eyes were open, but I couldn't see anything. Where's Jason? Where's Annalise?"

They're just fine. Jason will be right back. Susan felt her heart skip a beat. "Do you think…?"

"Of course. It's getting worse. I'm scared."

"Honey, don't jump to conclusions. It could be the genetic thing." Susan remembered the letter sitting on her coffee table. "In fact, I may be closer than ever to having answers for you." A nurse walked into the room with a new IV bag.

"I see you've woken up," said the nurse. Susan noted a hint of surprise in her voice. Didn't she expect her to wake up? "How are you feeling?"

"My head hurts, and I'm really tired. What happened to my arm?"

"Your arm is broken. I'm going to get the doctor. He'll explain everything to you." The nurse hurried out of the room, giving Susan a nod as she did.

The doctor came in and Susan waited outside while he examined Lynette. Jason and Mike were still downstairs in the cafeteria. She tried calling them, but there was no service. A middle-aged man sat alone in the waiting room. She sat down next to him and felt words falling out of her mouth.

"My daughter just woke up. I'm so relieved. She had an accident. Couldn't see. She has this condition that's scary. She might be going blind. That's probably what happened. At least she's still alive. She's a detective you know. Westbrook Police Department."

The man didn't say a word. It was as if Susan was talking to herself.

Soon the doctor came back out.

"Well, how is she?" asked Susan.

"The fact she's awakened is great news, and she doesn't seem to have any memory loss. We'll run some more tests, but I'm cautiously optimistic."

Mike and Jason returned to the waiting area. Mike handed Susan a cup of coffee and a sandwich.

"Great news. Lynette woke up. The doctor just checked on her."

"Thank God," said Jason. "What did the doctor say? I have to get in there."

"They'll be running more tests, but at the moment things are looking up."

Jason ran over to Lynette's bed, while Susan told Mike what Lynette said about not being able to see.

"Don't go saying anything about that. We don't know what she's dealing with yet. You have to make that phone call to the Georgia Babes."

"I will. Let's say goodbye to Lynette and go home. I'll call on the way."

As soon as they walked in the door, Susan picked up the letter and punched the numbers on her cell phone. Her hands were shaking and she had to start over three times before getting it right.

"It's ringing," she told Mike. Her palms were sweating.

"Hello, this is Susan Wiles. I received a letter saying you had some information." She picked her cuticles. Was she understanding this correctly? "Yes, just a minute." She grabbed a pen and jotted down some information. "Thank you so much." Her legs were spaghetti and blood pounded through her veins.

"Well? Are you going to tell me or are you trying to keep me in suspense?"

"Mike," constricted words sputtered out of her mouth. "They found my birth mother."

Chapter 48

"Are you okay?"

"I will be. I'm going to call this number." Her fingers shook. She misdialed and had to start again. "It's going to voicemail." Her body relaxed. "I'll try later."

"Can I get you something? How about a cup of tea?"

"I'll get it." She walked into the kitchen.

"Mike, the window is cracked open again. This time I know I didn't open it." Mike ran in and examined it. "Don't touch it. Maybe there are fingerprints."

"Were we robbed?"

Mike checked the laptop and Susan's jewelry. "Nothing's missing. Maybe one of the cats managed to open it."

"Do you know how ridiculous that sounds?" said Susan. "Let's check outside." They opened the sliding glass door and checked the porch.

"Nothing looks out of place," said Mike. "We can walk around to the front if it makes you feel better."

Susan stopped dead in her tracks. "There. See?"

"See what?"

She pointed to the ground. "Footprints in the snow."

Mike followed the footprints. "They stop here. He must have parked a car right here in our driveway. I'm calling Jackson."

When Jackson arrived, he examined the prints and open window. He took pictures of both and tried to get prints off the window sill with scotch tape.

"No prints here. Must have worn gloves. Who do you think did this?"

"It wasn't a robbery. Maybe Rusty or Sophie know we're getting close to finding Caleb's killer. Could it be one of them?" asked Susan.

"Even if they knew we were on to them, what were they looking for? I'll go ask your neighbors if they saw anything."

"Wait Jackson. Maybe Lindsay Bateman. She's cuckoo."

"One step at a time. Let me get on this. Meanwhile, keep things locked up. I'm sure Lynette's told you that a million times."

"I always do, but the lock to that window is broken. I keep forgetting about getting it fixed."

"I'll take care of that right now," said Mike. He retrieved his toolbox from the porch.

Susan couldn't focus and forgot about calling her birth mother until it was too late. Getting the woman out of bed in the middle of the night wouldn't be a great start.

She went to the computer and searched. *Florida. This number is in Ft. Lauderdale, Florida.* Well, at least they were in the same time zone. Didn't people retire in Florida? Her mom would certainly be retired by now, right? Flights to Florida were relatively cheap from New York. She was getting ahead of herself. This could still be a dead end, or maybe her mother wanted to contact her to say she wanted no further contact. She felt another sleepless night coming on.

Susan's cell phone startled her awake. Light from outside peeked through the blinds and Susan realized she'd gotten at least some sleep. Did Lynette take a turn for the worse? She exhaled as soon as she heard Lynette's voice.

"Mom, I need you to come to Dansfield right now."

"What's wrong, Lynette?"

"I don't want to talk about it over the phone. I'll see you shortly." Susan reached across the bed and shook Mike. She explained Lynette's request and Mike called his boss to say he'd be late. Sheets of freezing rain pelted the roof.

"Great. The weather's going to slow us down," said Susan. Mike assured her that he'd drive as fast as safely possible. After a few minutes in the car, Susan began picking at her cuticles.

"Mike, can't you go a little faster?"

"The roads are slick. Stop talking. I have to concentrate on the road."

They made it safely to Dansfield and went up to Lynette's room. Susan felt relieved. Her daughter looked a hundred percent better than the day before. A mostly finished tray of food was on the night stand.

"Good to see you've gotten your appetite back," said Susan. "What's with that scowl?"

"Mom, I couldn't be more furious with you than I am right now."

"Why, Lynette? What have I done?"

"I asked you not to tell anyone about my condition. You promised. I trusted you."

"I didn't say anything."

"You didn't go blabbing out in the waiting room? Come on, don't lie to me."

"I may have, but I was talking to myself."

"Think hard. You were alone?"

"There was one guy sitting there. He wasn't listening to me. Looked like he was thinking about his own problems."

"That guy happens to be my boss. He came to see me. Boy, did he ever get an earful."

Susan wished the floor would swallow her whole. "Lynette, I didn't know. I'm so sorry."

"He knows I could lose my vision. He says I'm a danger to myself and others. He says I'm unfit for duty."

Susan figured after one look at Lynette with her splinted arm and gauze-wrapped head, he was already thinking that. He didn't need Susan's help to come to that conclusion.

"Lynette, you aren't going to be going back for a while anyway. You still have a lot of recovering to do."

"That's not the point. I could have at least returned to part-time desk duty in a few weeks. Now I'm on leave indefinitely."

Mike, who'd been observing the whole conversation, chimed in. "Susan, what did you do? You broke Lynette's confidence."

"Are you on her side? I didn't mean to. How was I supposed to know the man in the waiting room was her boss?"

"Now she has a big problem. Suppose it's nothing, just a genetic condition. She may lose her job over this. You should have kept your mouth shut."

Susan couldn't believe she was hearing this from Mike. "You're kidding, right?"

Mike rarely raised his voice, but now he was almost yelling. "You always have to butt in where you have no business. You just ruined our daughter's career."

"I can't believe I'm hearing this." She slammed the hospital room door and stormed into the elevator. She felt her blood pressure rising. Luckily she had her own keys. *Mike can find his own way home.* The roads were still slick. She had to drive so slowly that it was frustrating. Every muscle in her neck ached. On the way home, she received a call from Jason.

"Susan, it's me. I just talked to Lynette and she told me what you did. How could you? That was supposed to be kept confidential."

"But, Jason, I was just telling myself maybe that's why she had the accident. She told me she couldn't see right before she crashed. I didn't think I was doing anything wrong. Maybe it's better her boss knows. Do you think she should be driving under the circumstances?"

"She wasn't going to be driving for a while anyway. Not with that cast on her arm. I'm so disappointed. I thought we could trust you."

"Go to hell, Jason. I know I did the right thing. I may have just saved your wife's life." She pushed the end button so hard she was afraid she'd broken the phone. She grasped the steering wheel. *It's for the best Lynette won't be putting her life at risk. I can't believe none of them see it my way.* Then she leaned a little too heavily on the brake. Pirouetted in the middle of the street.

Oh no, this is bad. She felt like she was riding a roller coaster in slow motion. She took her foot off the brake and steered into the skid. A van, honking vehemently, nearly sideswiped her. Her car kept spinning until it hit a snow bank.

Now what am I going to do? I'm stuck and I'm sure not calling Mike or Jason for help. She wasn't far from town. Could she walk home? No, that would be really stupid. *I'll call Jackson.* She pulled her coat tight and wrapped the scarf over her nose and mouth. Her hands and feet were already numb from the cold. It wasn't long before he came to her rescue.

"Jackson. I knew I could count on you."

"Come on now, Miss Marple, what kind of mischief have you gotten into now?"

Susan hugged him hard and began to cry out her anger and frustration. She explained the whole situation to Jackson as he tried to dig her car out of the snow bank. He turned the key in the ignition.

"It's not starting. I'll call for a tow truck. Now about Lynette. She should have told me. I'm her partner. My life's in danger too, driving around with her. I'm really miffed at her right now."

"Then you understand?"

"I'm on your side. She shouldn't be on duty. They'll come around after they settle down and think it through."

The tow truck arrived promptly, surprising Susan. With the roads being slick, she'd expected plenty of accidents. Then again, maybe sensible people didn't venture out when the roads were bad.

"Come on. I'll bring you home," said Jackson. Susan slid into the cruiser. Jackson received a call from the station on their way back. By the tone of his voice, Susan could tell that it was urgent.

"Susan, I hope you don't mind but we have to make a stop on the way."

Chapter 49

The siren blared and Jackson pushed hard on the gas.

"Where are we going?"

"You'll see."

Jackson turned into a neighborhood which looked familiar to Susan. This was that Lindsay Bateman's neighborhood.

"Stay in the car. There's some sort of emergency," said Jackson. Susan ignored his request and followed him to the front door.

"Thank God you came," said Lindsay's mother. "Lindsay has flipped out. She said she had to talk to the police. I found your number on her desk."

"What's going on?" said Jackson.

"Follow me." She led them down the hall to Lindsay's bedroom, where Lindsay was throwing books, papers, even the blankets from her bed. "She started having this tantrum. I can't reason with her. All she kept saying was call the detectives."

"Lindsay, I'm detective Simpson. I'm here to help. Can you tell me what's wrong?"

Lindsay screamed and threw her pillow at him.

"Come on, let's sit down on the bed and tell me what's wrong. I'm here to help you."

Lindsay started pulling on her own hair and continued screaming. Then she kicked the desk with her fuzzy slipper.

Susan walked in. "Lindsay, remember me? Susan Wiles?"

Lindsay took a few deep breaths. Susan could tell she was beginning to calm down.

"That's it, Lindsay. Come sit down with me and Detective Simpson." Lindsay stopped kicking and let go of her hair. She followed Susan to the bed.

"That bastard. He was using me. I hate men. You know, don't you?"

"What do you mean?" said Susan.

"You know about men acting like bastards. Remember, he hurt your daughter. He left her."

"You mean Caleb Bartolo? Did he do something to you?"

"Not him this time. It was that other son of a bitch. Rusty."

"Rusty Sumter?"

"Yeah. He pretended he was my boyfriend. They lie. All of them. The devil lives in their souls."

"So tell me what happened?"

"The creep broke up with me. Said he didn't think things were working out. Dumped me just like Caleb did."

"Men. They don't know a good thing if it bites them on the nose. It's his loss."

"He's going to pay for this. This time I'm getting even." She turned to Jackson. "You have to arrest him. He's a thief, a two-bit crook."

Jackson scooted closer. "What are you talking about? Did you see him steal something?"

"I sure saw him breaking and entering. That's what they call it, isn't it? When someone gets in through a window and sneaks around someone's house? When someone fools around on a computer that doesn't belong to him?"

"Are you saying you saw Rusty do that?" asked Jackson.

"Sure did. And more than once. Satan controls him."
She clasped her hands and prayed, "Hail Mary, full of
grace...."

"Whose house did he break into?" said Jackson.

"Caleb's. Ha. He didn't know I was there. I thought
he was sneaking around on me with another girl so I
followed him. Wasn't gonna be played for a fool. Not
again."

"You followed him to Caleb Bartolo's house?"

"Yep. He took something out of the back of the
truck. Looked like a crowbar. I watched him stick it in
the window and jimmy it open. Then I snuck myself
over to peek in. He was typing something on Caleb's
laptop."

"Did you see what he was writing?"

"Too far away."

Jackson leaned in. "Did he take anything?"

"Nope. Just typed on the computer. Went back out
the window and I followed him back to his house."

"And then?"

"Then I went back home and went to bed. After I
wrote in my diary."

Susan chimed in. "You said he did that more than
once?"

"Yep. Two more times that I saw. The last one was
the night Caleb was murdered. We had dinner, then he
said he had to go home and do something for his Dad. I
followed him again, to make sure the bastard wasn't
lying."

"Did you see him leave the house? Was Caleb
inside? Did you see Rusty kill him?"

"Wish I could say yes, but Caleb wasn't home. His
car wasn't out front or nothing."

"Did you see anything else?"

"Nope. The light was on in the main house and the
farmer's car was parked in the driveway. Nothing else."

"You did great, Lindsay," said Susan. She gave her a hug. "You know you're better off without him. You deserve much better."

Lindsay again turned to Jackson. "You're gonna arrest him, right? You can tell him I turned him in. Put him in jail so he won't hurt no one else."

"Thank you, Lindsay. We'll get right on it. Are you feeling better now?"

"Yes. Better."

As they walked out, Jackson told Lindsay's mother to call Lindsay's doctor. Mrs. Bateman assured him that she would. Susan and Jackson got back into the car.

"Well, that seals it. Looks like Rusty is the one who killed Caleb," said Susan.

"Oh, no. We can't jump to that conclusion. Lindsay saw him at Caleb's the night of the murder, but she said Caleb wasn't home. I'm sure she would've been happy to tell us if she saw Rusty kill him."

"What was he doing on Caleb's computer?"

"We have it in the evidence room. Didn't find anything odd, other than the threats he e-mailed to Sophie."

"Rusty's father said his son was great with computers. Is it possible that he used Caleb's computer to write those threats himself?"

"Why would he do that? We were going on the assumption that Rusty and Sophie were still seeing each other. They were on the same team."

"Yes," said Susan. "On the same team. Exactly."

Chapter 50

Susan noticed several voicemails from Mike but chose to ignore them. She sent a message to Theresa at school asking her to pick up the baby on her way home and bring her over. She had no car at the moment and figured Mike had to wait for Jason to leave the hospital in order to get a ride. That could take a while. *Serves him right.* She replayed the conversation she'd had with Lindsay—the one about men being bastards. She found herself agreeing. Agreeing with a crazy lady.

Susan called her birth mother again. She didn't expect anyone to pick up and was surprised to hear a woman's voice on the other end of the line. She felt her throat get dry. Was this the moment she'd been playing over and over again in her mind?

"Hello, my name is Susan Wiles." She cleared her throat. "I got your number from the Georgia Babes Foundation. I…."

"Georgia Babes? Who is this?"

"I think I'm your daughter. I had a cheek swab done and the agency said they found a relative. They gave me your number." She couldn't summon up enough saliva in her mouth to swallow and felt herself choking.

"Let me catch my breath. I registered with the same organization. Had a cheek swab too. Is your birthday March 10?"

"Yes, it is." There was silence on the other end of the line. Then a tentative voice spoke.

"Susan." There was a pause. "Your name is Susan?"

"Yes, it is."

"For 62 years I wondered what your name was."

"Then, you are my birth mother?"

"Yes. I didn't know where you were. That was part of the deal. I didn't even know if you were still alive."

"Alive and kicking."

"And happy? Things turned out well?"

"My parents were great. I suppose I should be thanking you." Her hands were trembling.

"Susan, I don't want to do this over the phone. Where do you live?"

"I'm in Westbrook, New York. It's about 90 miles north of New York City."

"I'm down near Ft. Lauderdale. It's hard for me to travel these days. Is there any chance of you flying down?"

Susan didn't hesitate. "I'll be there as soon as I can arrange it. By the way, what is your name?"

"I'm Audrey. Audrey Harrison. After all these years I'm going to meet my daughter."

Susan's fingers were shaking as she ended the call. She sat down on the sofa next to Johann. Petting him helped her feel calm. She did it. She found her birth mother. She couldn't wait to meet her and find the answer to all her questions. She couldn't wait to tell Mike. Then she remembered she was mad at him. She wasn't going to call him. She went over to her computer and started searching for flights to Ft. Lauderdale.

When Mike got home, she gave him an icy greeting and simply stated that she would be leaving for Ft. Lauderdale the next day.

"You talked to her? You found your birth mother?"

"I don't feel like talking about it with you. In fact, I don't feel like talking to you at all."

"I'm still mad at you too. I can't believe you did that to Lynette. And by the way, where's the car?"

"It's being taken care of."

Chapter 51

Susan turned off the alarm clock and peeked out her window. The ground was covered with snow and large flakes fell from the sky. Her flight was supposed to leave in a few hours. She turned on the local news and her heart dropped when she saw how bad the weather conditions were. Flights were being delayed or canceled by the dozens. She checked her flight, and indeed it was delayed by several hours. When she tried to call the airport shuttle service to change her reservation, no one even picked up.

Mike hadn't said a word to her since last night. He made himself breakfast and mumbled, "Have a good trip" as he slammed the front door. Susan knew he wasn't daunted by driving in snowy weather. He simply took things slow and steady. As a matter of fact, he would have been her first choice as a ride to the airport, but not under the circumstances. Anyhow, she wouldn't have wanted to sit next to him in silence the whole ride and she was too angry to speak to him. She preferred to avoid a heated argument. She had other things on her mind.

Optimistically, she continued packing her carry-on suitcase as she watched the snow through her bedroom window. She even threw in a bathing suit. And a terry cloth cover-up. After all, women of a certain age shouldn't be flaunting too much skin, now should they? A sunny Florida beach sounded very enticing right now. She dug out her sunglasses too.

School closings and delays rolled along the bottom of the TV screen. *Oh no.* Her stomach dropped. 'Breaking news' announced the airport closure. After all this time, she was within hours of meeting her birth mother and now this. She felt sick. She wondered if Audrey would be as disappointed as she was about delaying their meeting. She sat on the bed for a few minutes, punched her pillow, and then called her.

"Susan, I'm so disappointed. I was looking forward to meeting you. I even took the day off. It's hard to imagine a snow storm while sitting here with the air conditioning on. It didn't even cross my mind that the flight might be canceled."

"I'll call the airline later and reschedule. I'll see you as soon as I can."

"Can't wait. See you soon."

Took the day off? That sounded crazy. Was her mother still out in the workforce at her age? She wished she had at least asked her what she did for a living. So many questions…

She called the hospital to check on Lynette's condition and was told that she would probably be going home in a few days. Then, she got a call from Antonio.

"Bonjourno, Susan. I had some new information to share with you. The school is closed today, but yesterday afternoon, Sophie came into my office very upset."

"Why? She's home safe and sound, and her abductor is dead."

"Turns out she received another threat,"

"A threat? But Caleb is dead."

"That's why she's upset. If she's still getting threats, then someone else has it in for her. Or, she thinks Caleb may have had a partner."

"Did she say who she thought this partner was?"

"She thinks it's her old high school sweetheart—Rusty Sumter. Look, I hate to keep bothering you about this situation, but rumors are already flying. A threating letter was slipped under her office door. Some of her officemates heard her scream, then they told their friends about it...you know the rest."

Susan and Jackson suspected Rusty of tampering with Caleb's computer to make it look as though Caleb was threatening Sophie. Lindsay Bateman placed him at Caleb's house and swears she saw Rusty using Caleb's laptop.

"Okay, Antonio. I'll see what I can do."

"Grazi. I knew I could count on you."

Susan called Jackson to tell him about this new development. He picked up on the first ring.

"Susan, I just called Lynette. She's doing much better and will be coming home soon."

"Is she still mad at me?"

"Well...yes. But she'll get over it. Give her time. You didn't do anything wrong."

"Jackson, I just spoke with Antonio Petrocelli over at Westbrook Middle. He says Sophie is still having problems. A threatening note was slipped under her office door."

"Yeah, I know all about it. Sophie Bartolo came into the station this morning. Braved the snow and everything. She accused Rusty Sumter of threatening her. Wants me to arrest him."

"Are you going to?"

"I don't have enough to arrest him, but I'll bring him in for questioning. I'm not sure I believe Sophie."

"Why not?"

"For one thing, the guy is a computer whiz. Why risk going over to the school to slip a letter to Sophie when all he had to do was send an e-mail? We know he can cover his tracks so I doubt he was worried about it being traced."

"Hmmm. And if he still had a thing for Sophie, why threaten her? He knew she was dating Mitch Coniglio," said Susan.

"I've got to go, someone just came in and I'm manning the office alone right now."

"We'll talk soon."

Susan finished booking her flight. She'd go to Florida over the weekend. The fare was significantly cheaper then anyway. She tried calling Audrey back, but it went straight to voicemail. *House is clean, don't want to drive in this weather....*She pulled a brand new cozy mystery off the shelf, and snuggled up on the couch with her cats to read.

Chapter 52

Susan kept her eyes closed and lay still when Mike's alarm went off. They still weren't speaking. She wondered if he'd make a full pot of coffee before he left, or use the Keurig to make a single cup. His taking Lynette's side over the medical thing still made her blood boil. After he left for work, Susan got out of bed and tried to call Audrey to tell her about her new travel plans. Audrey's phone went straight to voicemail. *That's strange. Why isn't she picking up? I was hoping she'd have called me back when she got yesterday's message.*

Susan was going to the high school to volunteer today, but made a stop along the way. She entered the police station and heard voices coming from Jackson's office. She decided to wait a few minutes before making her presence known. Was Jackson talking to Rusty? She hid behind the door.

"Mr. Sumter, some serious accusations have been made against you. Do you know a woman named Sophie Bartolo?" Rusty shrugged.

"Don't play games with me, Mr. Sumter. We know you and Ms. Bartolo had a relationship. You've known each other since high school, correct?"

"Yeah. So what? Hadn't seen her in years. Why are you asking me questions if you already have the answer?"

"Hold the attitude. And wipe that smirk off your face. Ms. Bartolo says you've been sending her threats."

"What? Why would I do that?"

"Maybe you wanted her back. Maybe after you killed Adam Bartolo and Sophie didn't respond to your knight in shining armor act, you got angry and decided to put some pressure on."

"I ain't talking no more." Rusty got up to leave Jackson's office. Jackson called after him. "You won't be so smug when we arrest you."

Susan announced her arrival by blocking the office door. Rusty exhaled with audible annoyance.

"Rusty, I wanted to thank you for your advice about the tub. Works great now. Lefty loosey, got to remember that for future reference." Susan stretched her hands across the doorframe, blocking his exit.

"Yeah, great. Now move so I can get out of here." Jackson mouthed the words 'good cop' to her.

Susan didn't move. Instead, she addressed Jackson. "What did you say to upset this nice young man? You police are all alike. I heard you making threats about arresting him."

Jackson assumed the bad cop persona, like he'd done so many times with Lynette. "This guy is a stalker and worse than that, a murderer."

Rusty had scowl lines around his mouth. "I ain't no stalker and I ain't no murderer. What are you talking about? Let me out of here right now or I'm calling a lawyer."

"Officer, I'm sure this man is just responding to the tone you've set," said Susan. She turned to Rusty. "You can't let this man falsely accuse you. Make him tell you what evidence he has and you tell him why you're innocent. I'm sure we can solve this without you paying a ridiculous fee for a lawyer. You know, I needed a lawyer last year and it wiped out my savings."

"Move," said Rusty.

"Officer, what evidence do you have against this man?"

"We have a threatening letter which was slid under Sophie Bartolo's door."

"I never set foot in that office," said Rusty.

"And who writes letters these days?" added Susan. "I'm sure you do all your corresponding on the computer, right?"

"We have a witness who saw you breaking into Caleb Bartolo's home on several occasions. You were there the night Mr. Bartolo was murdered," said Jackson.

"No f...ing way. You ain't gonna pin a murder on me." He tried to get around Susan but she stood solidly in his path.

"You better not leave town anytime soon. And work on your bucket list while you're still free because a jury is going to have you locked up for life. Maybe even getting the death penalty. How do you feel about needles, Mr. Sumter?"

"I didn't kill nobody."

"No, you didn't kill someone. You killed two people. Sophie Bartolo says you killed her husband, Adam. Says you fed him some pills and pushed him off a cliff. We have your fingerprints all over a prescription bottle. Blood pressure medicine with your father's name on it. You stole the pills and put them in Adam's lemonade. Sophie Bartolo already signed a statement. We even have a witness who saw you do it. Arrest warrant's being drafted as we speak."

"That bitch killed Adam, not me. And she killed Caleb Bartolo too."

Susan spoke up. "Maybe Sophie Bartolo is lying about this nice young man. He obviously didn't do it or he wouldn't be so upset."

"He did it. And Sophie Bartolo hired one of the best prosecutors in the state to take this case," said Jackson. Susan was amazed at how good of an actor Jackson was. Rusty was buying this, hook, line, and sinker.

"Officer, it sounds like a set up to me. Maybe Mr. Sumter here would like to tell his side of the story." Susan put her hand on Rusty's shoulder. Rusty jerked away.

"Last chance," said Jackson. "Come back into my office now, or you've got a few hours before we throw your ass in jail."

"Come on," said Susan. "Death by the needle—I've read that's really painful. Sometimes they mess up and it takes hours to die. Saw it on *Dateline*. This guy was foaming at the mouth and everything before he died." She led Rusty back into the office. "Tell your side of the story."

Rusty kicked the wall, then sat down. Susan handed him a cup of water from the cooler.

"I was at the house that night. I didn't kill nobody. I was in there setting up threats from Caleb's computer to Sophie."

"Why?" said Jackson.

"That bitch was blackmailing me something fierce. Made me write those threats from Caleb's computer. Made me steal a phone, too, and plant it in Caleb's house."

"Lindsay Bateman's phone?" said Jackson.

"Yeah, how did you know that?"

"We have our ways. What was Sophie Bartolo holding over your head? Must have been a doosey to get you breaking and entering."

"It started when her husband was alive. We had a thing going. Adam was beating her and spending all their money. She was going to leave him. I told her I'd take care of her."

"So you killed Adam?"

"No way. I heard about it on the news like everyone else. Told Sophie we had to break it off after he died. Wouldn't be right, her being a new widow, seeing me right away like that."

"Why did you steal your father's pills?"

"Sophie said she could slip them to Adam. They'd make him sleep and we could get some private time together."

"They're blood pressure pills. They don't make you sleep," said Jackson. Rusty looked genuinely surprised. His mouth dropped open and he gave himself a slap on the side of his head.

"Go on," said Jackson.

"After that, I didn't see Sophie for almost a year. Then out of the blue she calls and says she needs my help."

"With what?"

"She tells me Caleb Bartolo, Adam's brother, had hired someone to find out what killed him. He had some report. He even had pictures. Said he was going to go to the police with it and Sophie would be arrested for killing Adam. She said it was all a set up. I believed her."

"Is that why you helped her kill Caleb?"

"I didn't have anything to do with killing him. Sophie said she had my prints all over the prescription bottle and if I didn't help her, she'd tell the police that I drugged Adam and killed him. Then she got kidnapped. That's all I know. Why don't you go bring Sophie down here?"

"Write down everything you just told us and sign it." Jackson threw a legal pad across the desk to Rusty. "Then you can go. For now."

After Rusty was out of sight, Jackson gave Susan a high five. They were quite a team, she and Jackson.

They managed just fine without Lynette. She hoped he would tell her that.

When she got home, the mailbox at the end of the driveway was open. The mailman always closed it and so did she and Mike. They didn't want unexpected snow, or rain for that matter getting the mail wet. *Who left it open?* There was still a magazine and electric bill in the box, so it must have been left open after the mailman came. *Who was snooping through our mail?* She felt like caterpillars were crawling up her spine. She tip-toed around the perimeter of her house until she convinced herself that no one was lurking in the shadows.

After regaining her composure, she went inside and called Audrey, again to no avail. This time she left a message with her flight information, and a request. She asked if Audrey could fill her in on any pertinent medical information. She explained Lynette, Audrey's granddaughter, was having some health issues and might benefit from the information.

Mike got home from work, and told her Lynette would be released from the hospital the next day.

"Unfortunately, she won't have a job to go to, but she can be with Annalise. Daycare will have to go, what with them living on only one paycheck."

"At least Annalise will still have a mother."

Mike started up the stairs while Susan was talking. She called after him. "At least Lynette won't be putting herself in dangerous situations. Not that it seems to matter to you or Jason."

Susan turned on the TV and was watching the local news when she saw something completely unexpected. Rusty was being arrested for Caleb's murder. She immediately called Jackson.

"Jackson, what happened? I thought Rusty had cleared himself of Caleb's murder? Why are they arresting him?"

"After you left, I had a chat with Sophie Bartolo. Of course, she denied everything Rusty told us."

"Is that surprising?"

"No, but she led us to physical evidence tying Rusty into Caleb's murder."

"What evidence?"

"She said that Rusty had bragged about whacking Caleb over the head with a crowbar."

"Lindsay Bateman said Rusty broke into Caleb's house with a crowbar."

"Sophie said that Rusty kept the crowbar, kind of like a trophy. He told her it was in the back of his truck."

"Did you find it?"

"Sure did. It was under the floorboards with the spare tire. We lifted prints and blood off of it. The blood was Caleb's."

Chapter 53

Susan knew Lynette wouldn't want her there for her homecoming, but she couldn't stop being her mother, could she? She was sure Jason hadn't gone grocery shopping since Lynette's accident so she stocked her fridge and pantry. She couldn't stop thinking about Rusty's arrest. He had seemed so sincere yesterday when talking to her and Jackson. Why would he have been stupid enough to keep the murder weapon right there in his truck? She grabbed a wagon and started down the aisles of Shop Rite.

"Susan, fancy meeting you here."

"Sophie? I thought schools were open today?"

"They are. Antonio sent me to pick up some coffee supplies for the office."

Susan seized the opportunity to pump Sophie for information. "I saw that Rusty Sumter was arrested for Caleb's murder last night. I'll bet you're relieved that the case is solved."

"Who needs a murderer running around town? The streets of Westbrook are safe once again."

"You knew Rusty, right? I heard the two of you were long time acquaintances."

"We were high school sweethearts. Haven't seen him in many years."

Susan knew Sophie was lying. She was hiding something. "I'm so glad you came out of that kidnapping in one piece. You looked great on the news footage the day you were found, nails still intact, hair washed. I think you must have a metabolism like mine.

I was sure I was the only one in the world who could be held hostage and still be able to eat. Not even kidnapping would stop me."

"I had to keep up my strength so I'd be able to break free." Sophie looked at her watch. "I need to get back to school. Catch you later, Susan."

At Lynette's, Susan unpacked the groceries and straightened up. *Lynette would just die if she saw dishes piled in the sink and the bed unmade.* Susan wasn't sure if anger or hurt was winning the emotional battle inside her. She was out of there before Lynette and Jason arrived.

When she got home, there was a Fed Ex package on her doorstep. *What on earth could this be?* She took it inside and opened it. After reading through the papers, Susan felt as though she'd just received a brick of gold. She wiped away tears of joy and felt the corners of her mouth turn into a smile. She rushed back to Lynette's house just in time to see Jason helping her daughter into the house.

"Lynette, I need to talk to you."

"Go away, Mom. I don't have the energy for this."

"The doctor says she needs her rest. She'll call you when she's ready," said Jason.

"No, you need to see this." She waved the Fed Ex envelope in front of them. "It's really important."

"Five minutes. You have five minutes," said Lynette.

Susan handed Lynette the envelope.

"These are medical records," said Lynette.

"They are your grandmother's medical records. Read them."

Lynette started reading. Then she looked up at her mother.

"It says my grandmother had a benign eye condition." She continued. "This note next to it says:

'*This is genetic. It bothered me for a year or so, and never came back. Hope the information helps your daughter.*'"

"How did you get this?"

"Your grandmother. I found her, from that cheek swab I did. Her name is Audrey."

"You actually found her?"

"Lynette, this means you're going to be okay. You aren't going to lose your sight."

"And I still have a career. I can't believe it."

"I don't know what to say," said Jason. "Thank you."

"What a game changer. Mom, have you met her?"

"I was supposed to but the airport was closed because of the snowstorm. I was so disappointed. I'm going to Florida over the weekend, though."

"I'm so happy for you. I want to meet her too, as soon as I'm better."

"You get your rest and we'll have a family reunion soon. I didn't even tell her about Annalise yet. She doesn't know that she's a great grandmother. Unless she has other great grandchildren...I might have brothers and sisters."

Lynette gave her a hug. "Thank you for doing this. I'm sorry I got so mad."

"You have Annalise now so you should understand about being protective. Go. Get into bed. Get a nap. You'll need it before Annalise comes home. That little pistol never stops moving."

"The house looks great. What happened to all those dirty dishes? And I see you've been to the food store," said Jason.

"Just picked up a few things I thought you'd need. I'll call you later."

Chapter 54

Susan felt more relaxed than she had in weeks. She couldn't wait to get back home and try Audrey. This time luck was with her.

"Audrey, so glad I finally reached you. I got the medical records. Can't thank you enough."

"Susan?"

"You have no idea what this means to us, knowing Lynette isn't going to lose her sight. I left you the message about the flight information. You got it, right?"

Audrey's tone was icy, not warm like it was the last time they spoke.

"You got what you needed."

"Audrey? Hello… We seem to have a bad connection. Audrey?"

Susan felt her heart sink when the call ended. She wished she'd heard what else Audrey said. When she tried calling back, she got voicemail. What just happened here? Audrey was so friendly the first time they spoke. Had she reconsidered wanting to connect with her? No, she was just being paranoid. She'd talk to her again later.

"Hi, I'm home."

"Mike, you're early."

"Jason called and told me what happened. I can't believe you were able to hunt down those medical records. Our daughter isn't going blind. In a few weeks, Lynette can go back to work." He hugged her hard. She was still disappointed he hadn't supported her.

"I caused a problem and I fixed it. I can't tell you how relieved I feel."

"Me too. I knew it wasn't safe for Lynette to go back without knowing. I didn't want to admit how serious it was."

"I'll start dinner."

"I say we go out and celebrate. By the way, I almost forgot." He took a note out of his pocket. "This was on your windshield."

She took the folded note from him. "It says *stay out of it for your own good.*"

"What? Let me see that." Mike grabbed the note from her hands. "What does this mean? Stay out of what?"

"I think I know. I ran into Sophie Bartolo at Shop Rite. I may have asked her a few too many questions."

"Susan, what did you do?"

"They arrested Rusty Sumter for Caleb's murder. Mike, I don't think he did it. He told Jackson and me that Sophie set him up. She was blackmailing him."

"He told you and Jackson? We'll get back to that part later. Why were you questioning Sophie?"

"It's too convenient. Jackson questions her because Rusty implicated her. Then she pulls the murder weapon out of a hat. I think she planted it. I think she faked the whole kidnapping too. T.J.'s wife at the jewelry store said she had an ID bracelet engraved with the name Caleb. Conveniently, it's found in the parking lot the day she's kidnapped. She was trying to leave a false clue. One that pointed at Caleb."

"Maybe she gave Caleb the bracelet earlier."

"Then there's the witness who swears she ate dinner alone at the diner during the time she was missing. And she looked awfully put together the day she was found."

"Let's call Jackson and tell him about the note. She can't be threatening you. If she really killed Caleb, then this woman needs to be off the streets."

Chapter 55

Susan's head throbbed. She was upset by the threat from Sophie, but even worse, she didn't understand why her mother had suddenly done a 180. She checked her phone messages. Her heart held its breath. It was a threat. *Oh no, Sophie is stalking me now. What truth is she afraid I'm uncovering?* She yelled for Mike as she trotted down the steps.

"What is it? I was making us breakfast."

"Listen to this." She played the message. "*Stay away from danger or you will have regrets.*"

"I'm calling Jackson. He has to pick up this Sophie woman."

"Mike, let's just go down there. We'll probably have to sign a complaint or something."

"We could get a restraining order."

"Who would it be issued to? All we know is someone left two threats and we think it was Sophie. We don't have any proof that it was her."

They hurried down to the station and played the message for Jackson.

"I'll see if we can trace the call. Stay away from Sophie Bartolo. Meanwhile, keep your door locked and don't answer the phone if you don't recognize the number."

"Thanks, Jackson. You know I'm always careful."

"I have to get to work. I'll call you later," said Mike. He kissed Susan goodbye.

Susan unlocked her front door and had barely stepped inside when Sophie Bartolo barged in behind her. Susan dropped her purse.

"Sophie? What are you doing here?"

"We need to have a little chat. Seems you've been nosing around town and accusing me of Caleb's murder."

"I wouldn't say that. I'm naturally curious. Just a hobby. Ask anyone who knows me."

"You know what they say. Curiosity killed the cat."

Susan's pulse was racing. Sophie, potentially a murderer, had followed her home. She tried to swallow but couldn't.

"It's Rusty Sumter you should be digging up dirt on. He's still in love with me. Would do anything to protect me."

"Like what?"

"He knew Caleb had some trumped up evidence implicating me in my husband's death. His accidental death. I told Rusty how Caleb had been threatening to go to the police and to get me locked up. He knew how upset I was. And he didn't want me locked up away from him in prison."

"I don't believe Rusty masterminded this whole thing by himself. He may be good at plumbing and computers, but I don't think he's cunning enough to pull off a scheme like this."

"Then you don't know him very well." Sophie reached behind her and locked the front door. Susan grabbed the handle and tried to leave. Sophie pushed her back and pinned her against the wall.

"You have to leave right now." Susan was quivering inside but tried to muster up an authoritative voice.

"I'm not going anywhere," said Sophie. She pulled a gun out of her coat pocket. Susan's mind raced. She had to escape.

"You faked all of this, didn't you? Caleb couldn't have raised that paperweight over his head like you said. He had a shoulder injury. That's why he was home and not in Germany. If he didn't clobber you, then who did? Rusty? Mitch Coniglio? Lindsay Bateman?"

"I sent Mitch on a wild goose chase to get him out of the way. That man would do anything for me, just like Rusty. Mitch wasn't even in town that day."

"How about Lindsay Bateman?"

"That fruitcake? I could huff and puff and blow her right back to the psych ward. I had Rusty hook up with her to frame her for killing Caleb. He planted her phone at Caleb's for me."

"You faked the kidnapping, didn't you? You also killed Caleb. And Adam."

"Come on, Susan. We're going for a little ride." She pushed the gun against Susan's back. She led her to her car. Susan thought about falling to the ground and not obeying Sophie's order. Then she felt the gun butting through her coat and nixed that idea.

"Where are you taking me?"

"I think it's a beautiful day for a picnic, don't you? Drive." Sophie pointed the gun at Susan as she drove. "Turn here."

"So you faked the kidnapping so you could have an alibi when Caleb was murdered. You had that silver ID bracelet engraved with Caleb's name and left it in the parking lot so it would point to him as the kidnapper." Ice started pelting the windshield and the sky grew darker. Susan felt the road slipping under the wheels and feared another accident.

"Brilliant, right? I thought about being upfront and saying I killed him in self-defense. It was neater to simply frame Rusty for his murder. Otherwise he'd have expected to run off with me into the sunset. Killed two birds with one stone. Got them both out of the picture."

"And Adam? You killed him too?"

"Just a little push, no pun intended. Drugged him with Mr. Sumter's blood pressure medicine. He was whirling around like a top. Didn't take much to lead him to the edge of the waterfall. Didn't have to lay a finger on him. It was an accident. The police report verified it."

Susan recognized this road. She drove up the mountain edged with pine trees. Ice glistened on the road. Lake Minnewaska. So that's where they were headed.

"Park here. Now get out of the car." Susan's head throbbed and her legs felt like Jell-O.

"I thought I'd bring you to this lovely scenic spot. A fitting last look at the world."

Susan recognized the marker draped in rosary beads. "This is where you killed Caleb, right?" The sound of rushing water became louder with each step.

"He killed himself. I led the horse to the water. He chose to drink." Sophie nudged Susan closer to the edge of the waterfall. Susan didn't want to die. She dug her heels in. Sophie nudged harder and Susan approached the edge getting closer with each step.

"Sophie, don't do this. No one has to know. I won't tell anyone. Just let me go."

"Do you think I'm an idiot?"

"You could run away and no one would ever know." Susan felt herself losing traction as she backed up. Unable to maintain her balance, she fell to the ground, landing hard on her hip.

Sophie gave her a kick. "Get up."

Susan reached out her arm but found nothing to grab onto. The water sounded like an approaching train. Frozen bullets of ice stung her cheeks as they shot to the ground. When she looked over her shoulder, she saw she was only two feet away from the edge. Sophie lowered the gun until it pointed directly at her forehead. She took a deep breath and closed her eyes. She didn't want to die and prayed like she'd never prayed before. *Please, God. Don't let me die like this.*

In a flash, Sophie was knocked to the ground. Susan heard a thump. When she opened her eyes, Sophie was on the ground. The gun lay on the ice beside her. She saw Jackson sitting astride over Sophie. Then she watched him slap handcuffs on her. Mike and Lynette came running out of the police car.

"Mom, Mom, are you okay?"

"Thank God she didn't kill you," said Mike.

Susan hugged them until they couldn't breathe. Then she turned to Jackson.

"Jackson, you saved my life. This is enough to charge Sophie with murder, right?"

"We have our smoking gun. Had it before she grabbed you."

"Are you trying to kill me with the suspense?" said Susan.

"The blood found on the crowbar was Caleb's, but we found a fingerprint in that blood. We ran it through the database. All school employees have to be fingerprinted."

"And?"

Jackson cleared his throat "That fingerprint belongs to Sophie Bartolo. Her print was on the murder weapon. We got her dead to rights."

"We talked to Rusty and we've pieced together the whole thing. She killed Adam Bartolo because she was in financial trouble. She needed the life insurance money, and counted on her old boyfriend Rusty to take care of her."

As Sophie was led to the cruiser she said, "That's a lie. Adam fell off that cliff all by himself."

Lynette broke in. "We have a witness who saw Adam drinking lemonade, then acting dizzy and disoriented. That was right before he fell. Oddly enough, Rusty told us that you had asked him to swipe his father's blood pressure medicine. One of the side effects is dizziness."

"That was Rusty's idea. He killed Adam."

"Rusty has an airtight alibi for the day Adam was killed," said Lynette. "Adam's brother was on to you. When he got back from the military, he ordered a report which showed that Adam had Medipress in his system. Odd, since Adam had no history of high blood pressure. Caleb also tracked down a photographer, who witnessed Adam's bizarre behavior."

Jackson continued. "Caleb was threatening to bring the evidence to the police. That's when you came up with your plan. You faked your own kidnapping and framed Caleb. We know about the bracelet you planted in the parking lot."

"Caleb returned from duty early. He had an injured rotator cuff. There's no way he could have lifted the statue over his head to knock you out. You should have been more careful in fabricating your story," said Lynette.

"He did it. He knocked me out."

"You were never kidnapped. We have a witness who saw you at Donna's Diner during the time you were supposedly abducted."

Jackson continued. "The night of the murder, you snuck into Caleb's, opening the window with the crowbar Rusty forgot to take back with him after he broke in to plant those fake e-mail threats. You blackmailed Rusty into helping you with those. Lucky for you, the crowbar was laying there right outside.

Rusty had left it behind. Then you went in and hit Caleb over the head with it."

"I want a lawyer."

"Better late than never," said Jackson. He turned to the other officer, "Take her to the station and book her." He led her away in handcuffs.

"Who are you, Hawaii 5-0? Book her, Danno." Lynette laughed. "Dad, why don't you take Mom home? Jackson and I will go over to the Bartolos and tell them we have their sons' murderer."

Chapter 56

"Okay, Lynette. Tell Jason to put Annalise in her highchair. Dinner is ready."

"Lucky for you, I cooked tonight," said Mike.

"Jason, you're closer. Can you hit him for me?" said Susan. She helped Mike bring the lasagna and garlic bread to the table. "I made some noodles with butter for Annalise."

"Noodles with butter? That girl loves her garlic bread," said Lynette.

"I already know she gets her appetite from her mom," said Susan. "Still, tomato sauce is a bit rough for a toddler's tummy."

Mike interrupted. "So did Sophie Bartolo end up confessing?"

"She did. Tried to plea bargain, but we have too much against her. We're going for two counts of first degree murder."

"I'm sure the Bartolos are relieved that she's finally been caught," said Susan. Her cell phone vibrated on the coffee table. "Excuse me. It's Audrey. I'm going to see her this weekend."

Susan took the phone into the kitchen. "Audrey, I'm so glad you called back. I'll see you this weekend. What? Why? No, Audrey. Please." Susan put the phone in her pocket.

"Mom, are you okay in there?" said Lynette.

Susan sat back down at the table.

"What happened? Was it Audrey?" said Mike.

"That was odd. She sounded so strange. Audrey said not to come to Florida. Said it was too dangerous. Then she ended the call."

"Dangerous?" said Mike. "Is she worried about the plane getting hijacked or something?"

"Don't tease her, Dad. You know she's disappointed."

Annalise dumped the entire bowl of pasta on herself and squealed.

"Annalise, bad girl," said Lynette. "Food is for eating." She got a napkin and picked up the spaghetti from the floor.

"We left the diaper bag in the car," said Jason. "It has a change of clothes. I'll get it."

"No, I will. I need a little fresh air. Give me your keys," said Susan.

The air was bitter and Susan wished she'd thrown on a jacket. Lynette's car was parked at the end of the driveway. Susan was startled by a sound. When she turned to look, she only saw darkness. *Must have been the wind.* She retrieved the diaper bag, but when she went to lock the car back up, she was grabbed by a large figure in a black coat. Her heart stopped. A set of ebony eyes were the only features visible. The rest of the head was wrapped tightly in a wool scarf. She started to scream, but a gloved hand clenched her mouth shut.

"Don't scream," said the figure. "Get in the car."

Susan crawled into the back seat with this interloper. Her legs were shaking and sweat soaked her brow. She wriggled to try to free herself but couldn't.

"Don't be afraid. I'm not going to hurt you." The gloved hand moved away from her mouth and Susan caught her breath.

"Who are you and what do you want?"

"I'm not here to hurt you. Susan, I'm your brother."

ABOUT THE AUTHOR

 Diane Weiner is a veteran public school teacher and mother of four children. She has enjoyed reading for as long as she can remember. She has fond memories of reading Nancy Drew and Mary Higgins Clark on snowy weekend afternoons in upstate New York and yearned to write books that would bring that kind of enjoyment to her readers. Being an animal lover, she is a vegetarian and shares her home with two adorable cats and a little white dog. In her free time, she enjoys running, attending community theater productions, and spending time with her family (especially going to the mall with her teenage daughter and getting Dairy Queen afterwards). *Murder in the Middle* is the third book in her Susan Wiles School House Mystery series and she has plans for many more.